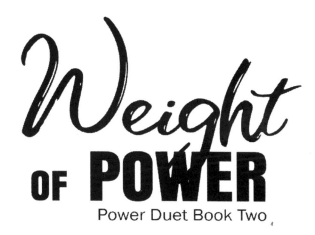

Power Duet Book Two

ANDREA BILLS

Weight of Power

Copyright © 2018, Andrea Bills

This is a work of fiction. Names, characters, places, and incidents are either the product of the author's imagination or are used factiously, and any resemblance to actual persons living or dead, business establishments, events, or locales, is entirely coincidental.
All Rights Reserved. No part of this book may be used or reproduced in any manner whatsoever without written permission of the author, except in the case of brief quotations embodied in critical articles or reviews.

Editor: Tayler Bennett
Cover Design: Amanda Walker

Never carry the burden of anyone else's expectations or perceptions of who they believe you should be. That weight is too heavy a burden. Instead own who you are and let that light shine. You never know who may be searching for it.

Chapter One

Austin

Austin wasn't sure where his day in the hellhole hospital was going, but it didn't seem good. He was tired of being poked at and monitored constantly for progress. He wanted out. He *had* to get out.

It had been a week since he had been injected with the serum to enhance his genetic makeup. The serum that they had absolutely no real knowledge on, and what affects Austin could suffer going forward. Austin, however, didn't want them to know that it had worked, so he lied when they asked him if he could hear better, see better, run faster he just shook his head. Anything they couldn't monitor by hooking him up to a machine, or see in his blood work, he lied about.

The top-secret unit he worked for had set up his lifelong best friend and fellow agent, Nick, to be the first one to take the drug. Fortunately for Nick, he had been able to avoid ending up in a hospital, so they settled for the next best agent, Austin.

Had Austin known what Dr. Hornerstern had been up to, he would have gladly taken the drug so that Nick and his wife, Hannah, could have avoided all of the pain they had endured. Instead they injected him when he had been drugged in between surgeries for burns covering most of his body after his own unit had tried to blow him and Nick to bits after they discovered the information about the serum. Austin should have been glad that the serum had ended up healing his burns, but it would have been nice to know before he went through the excruciatingly painful surgeries.

Instead it just fueled Austin's rage. Dr. Hornerstern had completely wrecked Nick and Hannah's lives. All so he could make himself feel more like a man with power. Austin shook his head; that wasn't power. What Austin had was power—power that made him feel reborn. A power that he would now use to avenge all the wrong that Dr. Hornerstern had dealt out. He would go to any length to see it through, even if it meant his own death. There wasn't anybody who needed Austin, so it made sense for it to be him to make the sacrifice.

He worked and that was about all his life consisted of. He had plenty of females willing to share his bed, but he never got close to anyone. He had been a product of the system since he was a teenager, so he didn't even have parents or siblings to give a damn. If the serum ended up killing anybody, he would be glad it was him and not Nick.

The nurse came in to check on him, reminding him that for now he was at Dr. Hornerstern's mercy. Austin would be damned if he would let the son of a bitch use him as some sort of super-agent for his own vendetta. The bastard had wanted a powerful agent who could go above and beyond, and that's exactly what he would get, but Austin would be his adversary. The toughest one the unit would ever go up against.

Austin felt incredible. He could hear things he knew he normally wouldn't have been able to hear. He was curious to see how fast he could run. Since he didn't want them to know how well the serum was working, he held himself back on the treadmill, but he could tell he was fast and his endurance would no doubt be almost endless. He didn't know when they were planning on letting him out, but he had plans of his own. Austin was anxious to see just what all he could do, and that meant he needed to get out.

He had made contact with an old friend from a small town in West Virginia who was going to bust him out. The location he had planned to hide out at would make the perfect place for him to discover more about his new talents. It was also close enough to Headquarters that when the time came, he could make his move.

Chapter Two

Headquarters

"What do you mean he's gone?" Dr. Hornerstern yelled.

He had shown up at the hospital anxious to see the progress they had made with Agent McGraw just to be informed that the agent was gone. Somehow the man had just walked out of a hospital swarming with agents whose only job had been to make sure that didn't happen; let alone the countless medical staff swarming the hospital.

"How did this happen? I need some answers immediately, and apparently I need some new agents!"

"Sir, we're not sure how just yet. We've asked for video surveillance to be pulled so that we can look through it."

"Have you asked the agent who was posted at his door? Surely he has some insight," Hornerstern was desperately trying not to strangle the young agent standing in front of him.

"Well sir... we did... but he was... he had stepped away for a minute to use the restroom, so we're thinking maybe that's when McGraw slipped out."

"A bathroom break, huh? So, all the work I have done over the past year, all the hell I have endured so that I can finally inject this serum to make *us* unstoppable! This agent takes a bathroom break and literally *pisses* the whole thing down the drain. A BATHROOM BREAK?"

Hornerstern felt like his head was going to start spinning any minute. How ignorant. How worthless were these new recruits that they left everything up to chance? This was why he had been so adamant that Nick MacKenzie be the first injected. He was an agent. McGraw was good, too; just as good. He was a little flakier, though. McGraw's head was big from years of working as a free agent amongst agencies. His loyalty wasn't to any one agency; it was to whomever he was contracted by at the time. He did have a loyalty to Nick, and that's what kept him working for Hornerstern as long as he had been.

He would do though. It would take some finesse, possibly even physical persuasion, to get him to agree to Hornerstern's terms. Hornerstern knew that Austin had been holding himself back during their testing. Hornerstern knew the serum was working on him. Now with Austin out there alone, he could fully utilize his skills.

Hornerstern knew just who he would be looking to use them against, too.

Hornerstern slammed his fist into a nearby wall causing all the agents in the room to jump.

"First off, I want the agent who was posted here last night brought to me immediately. Second, I want every last agent to be combing through this hospital asking anybody if they saw anything. If someone saw something, bring him or her to me immediately. Last of all, I want Agent Pepper and Agent Winland with me in the security office going over the feed from last night. Nobody eats, sleeps, or *pisses* without my permission. We must find Agent McGraw at all costs. On top of that, Agent MacKenzie is still missing. He may have helped McGraw," Hornerstern thought on it a minute realizing that the two could be together.

They had figured out what he was planning before he had been able to get to MacKenzie, and for some reason they both were very resistant; not the loyalty he would have expected out of Nick. It was that damn woman holding him back from his purpose in life as a superior agent. The power and the skills Nick was giving up because of her were unfathomable. Dr.Hornerstern should have killed her when he had the chance. Now she's shacked up with another one of his agents. A new recruit, but Dr. Hornerstern had high hopes for Agent Jared Tully as well. Maybe he needed to bring him in; Hornerstern had a feeling he knew where the other two were. No way that whore had let Nick out of her grasp so easily.

"Agent Winland, I need to know where Tully is immediately; I believe I'll pay a visit to him and his new girlfriend."

"Yes, sir."

Hornerstern started to walk out of the room and realized his agents were all still staring at him like lost puppies.

"Get to work. NOW!"

"Blubbering idiots," he muttered shaking his head.

Chapter Three

Nick

Nick woke up to the sound of his cell phone ringing. He rubbed his hand over his face before he reached over and grabbed his cell phone off the side table. After the explosion, he had found a nearby hotel that didn't ask a lot of questions, so he could stay close to Austin. Nick wasn't sure when the last night he had actually had a decent amount of sleep was, so he had to fight through the fog of exhaustion to focus on who was calling him.

"Nick, what the hell man?"

"What the hell what? You're the one calling me," Nick snapped.

"Where are you guys? Hornerstern has gone crazy; everyone is looking for you two. You better be hidden well. You may want to swap burner phones, too," Adrian said, in a whisper.

"You know damn well where I've been since the explosion, Adrian, so what do you mean where am I? Wait—did you say *you guys*?"

"Isn't Austin with you?"

"Austin is in the hospital as far as I know."

"Not as of this morning; he busted out some time last night. I just assumed he was with you."

Nick shot out of bed and started pacing.

"No. Shit. What's going on? Why wouldn't he have contacted me to let me know his plans? I could have helped. Where the hell is he?"

"That seems to be the question of the hour. He didn't have a burner on him, so I have no way to track him. They had talked about putting a chip in him after they injected him, but they hadn't gotten that far; they assumed he wouldn't be able to get out because of security. I really have no idea how he did it. The whole hospital has been on high security during the day and on lock down at night; there are agents everywhere."

"Damn."

Nick's mind was racing trying to think of where Austin could have gone. Who would Austin have trusted more than Nick to help him get out and go underground?

"Hannah! We need to get in touch with Jared. They're going to come after him and Hannah. I'll call you back, Adrian. Keep your ear to the ground; if they suspect you, you're going to have to get the hell out of dodge, too."

"Noted. Watch your six, man. Agents are everywhere."

Nick immediately dialed Jared's burner upon hanging up from Adrian.

"What's up?" Jared answered on the second ring.

"Is he with you?"

"Who?"

"Austin got out of the hospital last night. No one knows where he took off to."

"He hasn't contacted us," Jared replied.

"Get out, pack fast and light. I'm at a hotel not too far from you all. Don't drive here; hike through the woods. You'll be able to see where I marked my path. Do not answer any calls from anybody. Do you understand?"

"We'll be there within the hour."

Chapter Four

Austin

Two Months After the Explosion…

"You want any dessert or anything?"

"Nah, I'm fine. Thank you."

"You're welcome. Here's your bill whenever you're ready."

"Am I holding you up?"

"Oh no, I'm off the clock. I just came in to help the girls through the rush. It's technically my day off. I'll probably stay a while longer to help them clean some though. Stick around as long as you like."

"Working on your day off? That's no fun."

"Well I wish I could say I had grand plans and they were interrupted, but I don't have much of a life aside from working here, so it's no big," Nikki said with a shrug.

"That's a shame. I would imagine a girl like you would be pretty occupied when she's not at work."

Austin knew he had no business pursuing some local girl. He was in the area to lay low, but eventually he'd have to go back to the madness. For some reason, none of that mattered when he had seen her in the diner two months prior. Nikki was gorgeous, and he liked the way she showed her every emotion on her face. Part of his newfound skill set was that he had the ability to sense her emotions; not just hers—everyone's.

The first time he heard her laugh, his heard felt like it was going to beat out of his chest. The sound had been like nothing else he had ever heard. It had soothed him and at the same time petrified him. Having spent most of his life a loner, the fact that he felt so connected to her made him anxious.

Since he had been injected, his feelings and body weren't his own most of the time. He kept telling himself to stay away from Nikki. There was no telling what could happen to her if Hornerstern found out Austin had a connection to her.

Against his better judgment though, he kept ending up at the diner. Maybe it was all the increased training he was doing, and the seclusion of the cabin he was staying at that made him so drawn to her. His cell phone rang distracting him.

"Hello?" He answered as he threw a few bills on the table to cover his tab and a generous tip.

"I swear to God man, if you ever take off like that and not so much as leave me a crumb to follow again, I'm going to kill you with my bare hands. We both know I can."

How in the world had Nick tracked him down? Austin was grateful to hear Nick's voice, but he was worried if Nick could find him, so could Hornerstern.

"How did you get this number?"

"Come on, man. How long did you think it would take me to figure out you called Logan to hook you up with a cabin in his neck of the woods?"

"Well, I guess a lot longer than what it did. I didn't know if you'd even remember that; it's been a long time since your bachelor weekend."

"Two months is long enough; especially in a situation like this. I knew you'd want to be close, but undetectable. Don't worry; Hornerstern's no closer to finding you now than he was when you first gave him the slip. We need to meet."

"I'm just leaving the diner. Where are you at?"

"I'm at the cabin; get your ass here."

Once Austin pulled down the gravel road that lead to the cabin, he took note that there wasn't a car nearby for Nick, which meant he more than likely hitched a ride most of the way and then hiked the rest. Nick was a stickler for their training and was the best at going undetected. There wasn't a single light on in the house; which was impressive since they were well outside of the city, so when it got dark it got pitch black. Austin smiled to himself thinking about Nick sitting in the cabin all alone in the dark.

"Thank God you finally made it. It's dark as shit out here; I'm all about seclusion, but you need some solar lights or something. It's creepy as shit sitting here all by myself," Nick greeted Austin as Austin walked in and flipped the lights on.

"Hey man, I'm not running a Holiday Inn. You should have called first, and then I could have made sure I left a light on. I know how you get scared," Austin joked as he leaned in to give Nick the hug that men tended to give each other: one arm around the shoulders giving the other guy a good thump on the back while they clasped hands.

"I need to fill you in on some of what I learned, but first why the hell didn't you let me in on your grand plan to escape?"

"I wasn't even sure where you ended up after the explosion, or who all Hornerstern was watching. Logan was the safest choice."

"Two months though, man? Come on," Nick admonished him.

"Honestly, I didn't want anyone around until I knew I was safe. I'm still not even sure."

"Are you overly hostile?"

"No, but I can do some pretty wicked things. I'd hate to see you on the receiving end of them should I lose control."

"Well quit worrying about it. I'm here now. Let's get back to being partners, shall we?" Nick said his tone and expression serious.

"You said you've learned more about this serum recently?" Austin asked.

"I used my time in hiding—when I wasn't searching for you—reading everything I could get my hands on in regard to serums similar to this one."

"There are other serums like this one?" Austin asked.

"Not exactly, but the concept has been attempted before. During each World War there were scientists charged with developing a serum to enhance soldiers. No one was successful, but their research is interesting."

"How in the world did you get this information?"

"Adrian gathered it. That guy could run the world with his laptop. I can barely turn one on, so it all goes over my head when he gives me the details," Nick said with a shrug, leaning back into the chair.

Nick looked like hell. Austin had been on enough undercover missions to know that Nick had been living on the run since the explosion.

"Do you happen to have any of the research on you?"

"Yeah, I brought it. It's upstairs," Nick said, with a quick throw of his head towards the stairs.

"I just don't know what to do now. I mean Hornerstern's not going to quit looking for me. That puts everybody in danger right now. Speaking of which: where are Hannah and Jared? I'm sure they were at the top of the suspect list for hiding me."

"They're safe for now. Logan put them up in a cabin down the road. They agreed to wait until we spoke before they came over. I really don't know what we do now because you're right: they are never going to stop looking for you."

"Maybe I should just turn myself in?"

"Fuck that! They're going to use you like some sort of modern day gladiator. I don't think Hornerstern's intentions have ever been sincere with this project. He was too desperate to get this done; he wants you for something much more personal. We need to take him out."

"If we take him out someone else will just come for me. He's not the only one now who knows what I am and may want to use me for their own personal gain."

"You're right. Maybe for now our best bet is to enjoy our reprieve. We need to know more about what you can do. I take it you've been enhancing your new skill set?"

"I have. It's unbelievable really. Maybe it's time to call Jared and Hannah over and fill them in. They're a part of this, too, and they may feel differently. Especially Hannah; her life hasn't been her own for a while now; she may not want to sit in hiding any longer than she already has."

"She won't have a say. She has to stay where she is safe, and that's all there is to it," Nick said, with a bite.

Chapter Five

Headquarters

"Sir, I'm sorry to bother you, but I'm here with an update."

"Yes, come in, Chad. Have you found them; *any* of them?" Hornerstern was already rounding his desk when he noticed the agent was shaking his head like a nervous schoolboy.

"We can't seem to find them, sir."

"Always problems with you new agents; never solutions. How have we managed to let every person of interest on this case slip between our fingers? You agents are either in the pisser or standing around with your thumbs up your asses. You never have any progress for me; never any success. That's why I needed Agent MacKenzie for the serum. Of course, Agent McGraw makes a great candidate as well, but that's why it had to be them and not you all. You're worthless. I can't waste a drop of it on complete imbeciles," Hornerstern raged.

The more he ranted, the angrier he got and the louder he got. He slammed his fists on his desk in an attempt to control his rage.

"GET ME SOME SOLUTIONS!"

With that, the agent spun around and left.

Hornerstern paced his office for a while before he felt calm enough to sit down. He needed MacKenzie and McGraw so that he could follow through with his plans. He would have them under his control, so he could be the leader of the top agency in the government. He would name his price; if others wanted to utilize his assets, they would have to pay. That's if he would even be so inclined to take the job. Nowadays the government didn't pay shit compared to black-market type clients.

None of it mattered without McGraw, though. The new agents were spineless wannabes out of the FBI and CIA. He had waited so long for agents like McGraw and Mackenzie, he was afraid he'd never come across agents of their stature ever again.

Where were they?

With the skill set they possessed, they could be anywhere. Going into hiding for months was nothing for them and finding them would be nearly impossible. Hornerstern then wondered how Austin was feeling. Did he know how much power he had? Had he figured out all the details with his newfound greatness? If he had, then Hornerstern might never catch him; not without someone just as capable to go in after him.

With that thought, Hornerstern perked up. Maybe someone wouldn't necessarily need to go in after McGraw, if Hornerstern could draw him out. He searched for his cell phone, frantic to put his plan into place.

"Hello, Dr. Hornerstern," his associated answered.

"I've been thinking; you said you had a drug available, when we first discussed the serum, that was capable of distorting a person's thoughts. I need to know more about this drug immediately," he said in lieu of any pleasantries.

There was a pause before he replied.

"Dr. Hornerstern, I'm aware of the mishap at the hospital. I don't know if I'm prepared to give you yet another experimental drug, seeing as how we don't have any information from the first one. These drugs are dangerous and not to be used frivolously."

"Yes, I know, I lost the last experimental person, but I'm thinking this may be the key in getting him back and getting us another candidate to study as well."

A sigh filled the phone.

"This will be the last favor until I get results. I'll send you over my data on the drug."

"Perfect. I'll be in touch after I've read through your information, and I have the person ready for injection."

Chapter Six

Hannah

"This place is great," Hannah yelled to Nikki over the music.

"Yeah it's not bad for a little town," Nikki, the waitress Austin had been dragging them all to see for a week, yelled back.

"Absolutely. You wanna go dance?" Hannah asked her.

The two women were fast friends. Hannah felt like it had been forever since she had a girlfriend. Even though they didn't know each other well, it was nice to be out at a bar with Nikki there. It made her feel somewhat normal. Hannah shuddered a bit at the word. If being on the run with her ex-husband and her new boyfriend, both of whom she still loved was considered normal.

Nikki nodded and took Hannah's extended hand as she led her out onto the dance floor, beers in tow. They moved in and out of the crowd on the dance floor. Hannah felt both Nick and Jared's eyes on her the entire time. Her skin prickled with excitement. She knew she shouldn't respond to both of them, but she couldn't stop herself. Hannah and Nick had an age-old attraction that was embedded in her soul. When he was near, her body wanted to be close to him, to feel his calloused hands on her skin.

The pull to Jared was no less as potent. Jared was the healing anecdote to her shattered heart. She craved him. Hannah didn't want to love them both, but she wasn't sure how to stop. Having them in the same place with such a sexually charged atmosphere was wreaking havoc on her already strained nerves.

The song came to an end, just as another one immediately filled the room. Hannah's eyes floated across the bar back to where the men were all seated. Jared was no longer with them, but Nick was still there, his eyes locked on her. Chills broke out over Hannah's body. Nick's eyes were dark pits of pure desire. His body radiated lust so strongly she could feel it even where she stood. Hannah wanted to look away and seek out Jared, but Nick held her captive.

The dark shirt he had on didn't leave anything to the imagination, as it pulled tight across his chest. It was tucked inside of his dark jeans that clung to his powerful legs. Hannah knew everything he had to offer; she knew how every single one of his hard muscles felt under her fingertips. How his breathing changed once he was inside of her. Nick stood up and made his way to her. Hannah held her breath. She knew she needed to find Jared, and to break the spell between her and Nick.

The closer Nick got though, the more entranced she became. Her skin was flush with anticipation when Nick finally closed the distance between them. His arm wrapped around her waist and pulled her up against him. Nick's hips moved effortlessly with the rhythm. Hannah moved in turn, as she inhaled his scent. His smell was toxic.

"Nick," she whispered.

"He's outside," Nick growled.

"I shouldn't still want you," she confessed.

His hand started to snake up the back of her shirt when gunfire erupted in the bar.

Nick immediately yanked back and pushed Hannah behind him. Nikki took off toward Austin. Hannah scrambled to keep up with what was happening. The gunfire continued in rapid succession as Nick pushed her further back into the bar, his body a shield from the chaos behind them. She pushed her way through the crowd. The back exit of the bar was overrun with people.

Nick jerked her in a different direction, and she had no choice but to follow him.

"Open the door to the bathroom, Hannah," Nick ordered.

Once she had it open, Nick pushed her all the way inside before turning to throw the deadbolt. Then he moved to the far side of the bathroom and climbed on top of one of the sinks, so he could reach a window just overhead. Hannah followed him, wishing there was something more she could to. After a few seconds of Nick struggling to open the window, he pulled his shirt off, wrapped it around his hand, and then sent his fist through it. Glass flew everywhere.

"Oh my God," she gasped.

"It's okay," Nick said, as he began clearing as much glass from the frame as he could.

Hannah knew what Nick was going to ask her to do. She locked down the panic that was threatening to consume her and tried to focus. If she didn't get out of the bathroom, Nick wouldn't, and she wasn't prepared to bury the man; *again*. Jared was outside somewhere as well, and she needed to get to him and make sure he was okay.

"Okay, Hannah. I need you to go out the window. Austin is below; he'll catch you."

Nick jumped down, and when Hannah didn't immediately move, he gave her a little shove. The gunfire had stopped, but the sounds of the chaos on the other side of the door were terrifying.

"Hannah you need to go; you're putting everyone in danger by hesitating."

Anger seared through Hannah. She launched herself up onto the sink, feeling Nick's hands behind her legs in case she fell. She peered down through the window and saw Austin and Nikki below, but no Jared. Hannah didn't give it another thought as she pulled herself through the window and dropped down toward Austin.

The remaining glass tore at her stomach, but she stifled her scream. When Austin caught her, he was careful not to touch her stomach as he sat her down next to him. Nick was right behind her, somehow managing to land on his feet. She didn't have time to inspect the gashes marring his perfect body.

"You know anything useful?" Nick asked Austin.

"I don't know exactly who it is, but they're definitely from Headquarters. I recognized a voice. We need to go. Where's Jared?"

"He knows where the rendezvous point is; we need to move," Austin said.

"We can't leave him," Hannah cried as Nick shoved her along behind Austin and Nikki.

"Hannah, he's trained. He knows where we're headed; he'll get there," Nick assured her.

Hannah hoped Nick was right. They all piled into Austin's truck, and nobody said a word as Austin drove the truck past the turn off to the cabin. He kept driving north and as darkness began to fall outside, it felt like an omen to the group of the coming days.

Chapter Seven

Headquarters

"Tell me you managed to finally succeed at something."

"Yes sir, we have one of them in custody—Tully."

"Ah, the boyfriend. That will be perfect actually. Agent Winland, you've done excellent work. Drinks are on me once we get Agent Tully situated on his new assignment."

"Thank you, sir. We'll be there in thirty minutes or less."

Hornerstern hung up the phone and opened his desk drawer. He pulled out the bottle of whisky he kept stored there and took a celebratory shot. Now he just needed to call his associate, so that he could administer the drug to Agent Tully. If all went correctly by the week's end, he'd have McGraw back and possibly even MacKenzie. The three agents together would make a hell of an army.

He pulled out his cell phone and scrolled through contacts until he came across the one he wanted.

"Yes, Dr. Walker, please."

"Dr. Walker speaking."

"Hello, it's Dr. Hornerstern. My agent will be ready to have the injection administered by this evening if you would be available."

"That soon? I hadn't quite had a chance to see if there would be any adverse reactions from mixing the two injections. I was hoping to run some more tests. Is there a reason for the urgency?"

"Well, yes actually. I can't discuss the details with you, but since you're doing us such a big favor on short notice, I will divulge that we are dealing with a time sensitive terrorist threat. We desperately need this agent enhanced to help our tactical team neutralize the situation."

"I see. Okay. I will see you as soon as Pittsburgh's rush hour allows then Dr. Hornerstern."

"See you then Doctor."

Hornerstern hung up the phone. The doctor was becoming a nuisance. Hornerstern had wanted a more willing partner, instead he had someone who questioned his every move and required more information than he wanted to divulge. What Hornerstern needed was to get his hands on the serums for himself, so that he could administer them as he saw fit. Then he had a thought: the guy he had snagged from the IT department who had been helping McGraw and Mackenzie was in holding down the hall. The man's loyalty was up for question, but that was nothing a gun to the head wouldn't solve. Hornerstern made his way down the hall to have a chat with his newest traitor.

"Hello Adrian."

The agent didn't say anything, his eyes filled with anger.

"It seems were at a bit of an impasse. See, I should kill you for helping my agents stay hidden from me, but you did end up helping me in the end, so we've got some wiggle room for a negotiation."

"I'm not interested."

"I think you will be," Hornerstern said, as he pulled the gun out of his holster and aimed it at the man's head.

"Do it," Adrian seethed.

"You know the doctor who is providing the serums? You're going to hack into his server and find out exactly where he's holding the rest of it."

"Are you deaf? I said shoot me. I will not help you."

"How's your sister doing these days?" Hornerstern asked.

He had done his research on the man. The only person in Adrian's life was his twin sister. A twin sister, who Hornerstern could easily get his hands on, if he needed to. There was an agent tailing the woman, just waiting for the call.

"You son of a bitch. I'll kill you if you so much as set eyes on her."

"Tsk, tsk. That's no way to speak to your superior. Besides, I've already had eyes on her. With one phone call, I can get my *hands* on her. The decision's yours."

The agent struggled against his restraints momentarily. The attempt was in vain, though. Hornerstern waited.

"Fine. I'll need access to my laptop."

"There's a good boy."

Hornerstern untied him and led him to an office that adjoined his own. Then he paged for someone to bring Adrian his laptop.

"If you so much as even think about contacting any one, or leaving this building, I'll kill her—slowly."

Chapter Eight

Nick

Nick's phone rang, causing everyone in the hotel room to jump. They had arrived in a hotel just outside of Pittsburgh late into the night. Everybody was run down and tired, but nobody could sleep; not with Jared still missing and no updates from Adrian.

"What's happening?" Nick said in lieu of a greeting.

"Hornerstern has Jared. I'm sorry. They took my laptop and me. That's how they found you guys."

"Where are you now?"

"I'm still at Headquarters. Hornerstern is dangling my sister in front of me as leverage. I'm gathering information on the doctor who created the serum; Hornerstern is going after it. Apparently, the doctor's been a bit stingy."

"What does Hornerstern want with Jared?"

"I don't have an answer to that. I have to go."

The call was disconnected within seconds. Hannah slumped forward. She had been sitting next to Nick, leaning her head close to the phone so that she could hear what Adrian said. Nick wrapped an arm around her, offering what little bit of comfort he could.

Between his lack of sleep and the emotional whirlwind of handling a completely distraught Hannah, he wasn't firing on all cylinders. He wanted to ease her pain, but he also didn't want to seem like a vulture coming in to pick at the pieces with Jared gone. Hannah didn't deserve to have Jared taken from her. She had made her choice, and she had chosen Jared, so Nick would do everything in his power to bring him back to her.

Realizing that no one else had heard what Adrian had said, Nick filled them in on the situation.

"I should just go and turn myself over in exchange for Jared and Adrian's sister. This is all because Hornerstern wants me. He won't stop, either," Austin said.

"I think we need to get some sleep before we try to think on this anymore," Nick stated as he made his way to the door that adjoined their two rooms.

Hannah stood to follow him, but then she stopped. He could tell that she wasn't sure what to do. Austin and Nikki weren't really paying attention to them, already lost in an argument of their own over Austin turning himself over, so Nick grabbed her hand and led her into the room.

"I'll set my alarm for an hour, and then we'll figure out how the hell to get Jared back."

"You're going after him?" She asked, her voice and her face showing her shock.

Nick rested his hand on the side of her face.

"You chose him. I won't let you lose him."

"I can't believe you would do that for me."

"For you, I would do anything; I would look into the eyes of the devil and give him my soul."

"Nick," she whispered.

He shook his head.

"It's okay Hannah. Rest."

She nodded and lay down on the bed. Nick took up residence on the chair. Being so close to Hannah made him itch with the desire to touch her; especially knowing she was hurting. He wanted to wrap her up in his arms and comfort her. He knew he was a pig for thinking those thoughts, knowing she was upset over losing Jared. The other man. The man who she had chosen over Nick.

Nick flexed his hand, opened and closed, as he thought about the different scenarios that could play out. How each one affected Hannah. How each one of them affected *him.* Sleep finally consumed him.

Nick's phone rang waking him sooner than he had planned. He checked the caller and it was blocked which made the hair on the back of his neck stand up. He checked on Hannah; who was still asleep on the bed. Nick slipped outside to answer.

"Hello?"

"Awe, yes. Agent Mackenzie. So good to hear your voice and know you're not dead. It was very careless of you not to be in touch with me, don't you think, Agent?"

As soon as Nick recognized the voice he muted the call and banged on Austin's door.

Austin emerged looking grumpy, but once Nick showed him his phone, he slipped outside as well. There was no need to put the phone on speaker; he knew Austin could hear perfectly.

"I don't think so, sir. Are you upset that I'm not dead or that you couldn't inject me first?"

"That's a tough question, Agent. I had high hopes for you, but it seems that those hopes have been misplaced. I'm assuming my newest prodigy is close by, hmm?"

"Yes," Austin answered.

"Hello, Agent McGraw. How are you feeling?" Hornerstern laughed on the other side of the phone and the sound made Nick's skin crawl.

Nick couldn't imagine how he had worked for the man for so long and never realized what a psychopath he was.

"I digress, though. You're probably wondering how I got this number and why I'm calling. Well the first question is easily answered; yes, I know you've been getting information through Adrian in IT. I also know you probably want to know what I have planned for Agent Tully. I thought before you risk your pretty little necks with some half assed escape plan, I would just let you know that it's pointless."

"What do you want? If this is so pointless, then there has to be a reason for your call."

"Point? No, there's no point. I just like to gloat. You two know that I hate losing, and after a few mistakes you may have thought you had me, but alas you don't. See you soon boys."

With that the call was disconnected.

"What the hell?" Austin growled as he ran his hands through his hair.

"We need to get to Adrian's sister, and make sure she's safe. Then we need to work on extracting Jared and Adrian," Nick said.

"There's no need; she's safe. Jared, on the other hand, needs our help." Both men turned to find the IT agent approaching them.

"Jesus, it's good to see you, man. Hornerstern just called to mess with our heads; does he know you're gone?"

"It shouldn't be long before he finds out."

"What do you have on Jared?"

"Nothing, but I still have my ghost tap on Hornerstern's office. No time like the present to find out right?"

"Thank God for you computer nerds and your ghost shit that the rest of us don't understand."

"I'll take that as a compliment."

The guys all shoved into Austin's room where Nikki was already up and brewing coffee.

"Nikki, this is Adrian; he's the IT guy who's been helping us. This is Nikki, she's a friend who's got caught up in all of this mess."

"Typical field agent; we're trying to save your ass, you're out getting a piece," Adrian laughed.

Nick grabbed Austin's arm before he could grab Adrian's throat. He knew the comment would hit Austin the wrong way.

"I didn't think you computer guys ever emerged from your parents' basements?" Nikki quipped, easing the tension in Austin.

"I think I'll like it here; everyone's so welcoming when you've been saving their asses left and right."

"We do what we can. I'm going to go check in on Hannah," Nick said.

"No need. I'm up," Hannah said, as she came in from the adjoining room.

"Jared?"

"That's what Adrian's working on now."

Everyone fell silent as Adrian began to work. Nick watched Hannah, who was pacing the floor. She was just as beautiful as she had ever been. He hated that he had subjected her to the life of an agent's wife. Had he known all those years ago this is what she would have to endure, he would have never signed the fucking contract.

"I'm in," Adrian whispered.

When Adrian turned around to look at them, Nick could see the horror on his face. Nick jumped up and made his way to the computer. Hannah was close behind him. When he saw what Adrian had seen, he turned and grabbed Hannah by the shoulders.

"Hannah."

"Nick, get out of my way."

Nick's shoulder slumped as he did as she asked and moved to the side

Hannah took a step closer to the screen and stopped; she slowly extended her hand to touch it as silent tears fell down her face. Jared was strapped to a hospital bed with two IVs going in him. Nobody had to guess what one of those IVs was filled with. Nick prayed the other one was just fluids.

Nick slammed his fist into the wall sending dry wall everywhere. When he looked at Austin, he was a hum of energy; every muscle was tight in anticipation, and his face was solemn. Nikki went and put her arm around Hannah's shoulder and guided her to the edge of the bed to sit.

Adrian returned to his place in front of the laptop and was focused on studying something as everyone else let the shock settle.

"What is the second injection? Adrian, can you zoom in?" Austin asked.

"I can see what it is; I just don't know what it's for. I'm trying to look through Hornerstern's email and text messages right now to see what I can find."

All of a sudden, Austin collapsed to his knees. His breathing was heavy, and his eyes were glowing blue. Nikki stood and rushed to his side, but Nick stopped her. With everything they had been doing to see what Austin's capabilities were, his eyes had never glowed. Austin's body was shaking as if he were barely containing his rage. His eyes were fixated on the computer screen. Nick tried talking to him, but Austin remained incapacitated. Nikki finally pushed passed Nick and kneeled next to Austin.

"Austin?" She asked, tentatively.

Austin still gave no response. She touched his shoulder; Austin jerked away from her touch. Nikki looked to Nick for guidance, but Nick wasn't sure what was happening.

"Adrian, do you have any idea what's happening to him?"

Adrian jumped back up from the screen, pulling Nick's attention to the laptop. There on the screen, Jared was no longer lying in bed; he, too, was on the floor on his knees with blue glowing eyes and looked like he was desperately trying to hold onto his rage as well. Nick looked back over at Austin and then the screen. The two were somehow connected and were having some kind of weird reaction to each other.

"What the hell?" Adrian whispered.

Chapter Nine

Austin

Austin picked Nikki up and sat on the bed with her in his lap as he nuzzled his face in the crook of her neck and took deep breaths. He was amazed the woman wasn't running for her life. Even though they had flirted for months while he had been in hiding, it wasn't as if he had told her about his abilities. No matter how many hours he had spent sitting in her section at the diner, being shot at on their first date was probably a deal breaker. Austin berated himself for having asked Nikki to go out with them, but there was something about the woman he couldn't stay away from.

"I was just wondering why you haven't ran for the hills."

"It's been a long time since a man has had any effect on me. There's something about you. I want to be here; besides after getting shot at last night I figure you're my safest bet."

"I'm sorry. With everything Nick's been through, you'd think I would have known better," Austin said, rubbing his eyes with his finger and thumb.

"I know it's none of my business, but last night it seemed like there was something going on between Hannah and Nick. I thought she was with Jared?"

"It's complicated, but the cliff notes version is Nick and Hannah were married Nick had to fake his death to protect her, Jared came into the picture to protect her, and they fell in love. Then Nick had to reveal himself, and now here we are. One big, happy fucking family," Austin sighed, dragging his hand through his hair.

"Wow! So, Nick faked his death to protect her? I don't understand."

"What we do is dangerous. Having outside interests isn't really an option, but Nick couldn't leave Hannah. They had been together all through high school; she's the love of his life. We had a bad deal, and Nick thought she was in danger, and the only way to get the target off of her back was to make everyone believe he was dead. It almost destroyed Hannah."

"Not as much as him coming *back to life* did I'm sure. I couldn't imagine."

"You haven't asked about me yet?" Austin questioned her.

She shrugged and stood up and walked over to lean against the dresser.

"If you tell me, does it mean that I'm going to end up like Hannah? Attached to a man who I can never be with?"

"I don't want it to. I should tell you to run. After the first time I saw you in the diner and felt the attraction I had for you, I told myself to never go back there again. Instead, I went back day after day. I just wanted to hear you laugh; it calmed me in a way I have never experienced. I can't explain it."

When she didn't say anything, Austin stood up and began to pace. He wasn't sure he even really understood what he had become well enough to explain it to her. Austin was also still not completely sure she wouldn't run. He was a selfish bastard for wanting her to stay.

"I was injected with a serum the government has been working on to enhance the human body."

Her eyes widened briefly, and then she let out an exaggerated breath.

"So you're like what, Captain America?"

Austin looked at her quizzically and then busted out laughing. The analogy wasn't one he would have ever used, but it was probably the most accurate way to describe him. The idea of him in the tight spandex outfit was what was causing him to laugh.

"I suppose that's one way to look at it."

"He was always my favorite Avenger," she said, her eyes dancing with mischief.

"Is that so?" Austin asked, grabbing her by the waist and pulling her up against him.

Her body fit against his perfectly. Everything else ceased to exist. It was just them; alone in a hotel room. Austin lifted her up, and her legs wrapped around his waist. His hands instinctively went to her hips cementing them against him. Austin claimed her lips; gently at first, but once she gave him access, he demanded more. Nikki met his strokes with her own; she moaned with pleasure as he moved away from her mouth and began to pepper kisses down her neck, stopping every so often to suckle on her skin.

Before things could get too out of hand, Austin pulled away from her, leaning his forehead against hers.

"Another time, another place," she whispered.

Chapter Ten

Hannah

By the time everyone was awake the next day, Adrian was set up and tapping into his access to Headquarters. What he found once he pulled up the security footage made Hannah's knees weak. In the other room, Hannah stared at the computer screen watching Jared thrash about, throwing things and tearing apart anything he could get his hands on. He was in a complete rage, and the orderlies weren't having any luck catching him to strap him down. She looked over at Nick. He and Adrian were deep in conversation overtop of another laptop trying to get answers on what else had been given to Jared.

Hannah turned to Jared and saw that he was now up close to the camera looking directly at her. He was completely still. She had never seen anybody stand that still in her life. She was afraid to break eye contact with him like it would set him off again. He looked every bit the predator and not in a sexy way. Jared was trembling with anger and looked ready to rip something limb from limb. The hair on the back of her neck to stood up. His mouth started to move, and she realized he was talking.

"Adrian, how do we get the volume to turn up? Hurry; he's saying something."

Adrian rushed over and cranked the volume, and Jared's voice filled the room. Austin burst into the room, but never said a word as he stared at the screen.

"I know you're out there. I'm coming for you, and I'm going to kill you. You killed her! You took her from me, so now you have to pay. Can you feel me? Feel my rage and my hatred?"

"Who is *she*?" Hannah said.

"You. He thinks you're dead, and he thinks I'm the one who killed you," Austin replied, his voice harsh.

"How? Why? I'm here. Can we talk back to him? Can he hear us? I'm alive Jared," Hannah was all but screaming at the computer. She didn't know what would happen if Austin and Jared went toe to toe, but it wasn't something she was prepared to stand by and let happen.

"He can't hear you, Hannah," Nick said, softly.

"How do you know any of this?" Adrian asked Austin.

"I'm not sure how to explain it, I just know. I know what else they drugged him with. It's a mind alteration drug, and they've convinced him that I've killed Hannah. They even altered the image of Hannah in his mind so that if he would see you, he wouldn't know or believe that you are his Hannah."

"This can't be happening. Austin, surely you can convince him I'm alive," Hannah demanded.

"How are they connected?" Nick asked Adrian, talking about Austin and Jared.

Adrian didn't answer as he frantically typed away on his laptop.

"This is crazy," Nikki huffed as she slumped onto the couch.

"Shit," Adrian stammered.

"The reason Austin and Jared are connected is because they didn't just inject Jared with the serum, they injected him with serum extracted from the blood samples they took from Austin."

"That still doesn't make sense. If you get a blood transfusion, you don't become linked to the person who donated," Nikki said.

"No, you don't because normal blood isn't spiked with genetic enhancement serum. This is the only explanation: Austin's DNA is interlaced with the serum it's part of his genetic makeup now. They more than likely thought they had separated the genetic enhancement serum from Austin's blood, but they didn't. Had they ran any tests at all on what they pulled from Austin's blood they would have seen that they were injecting Jared with serum that had already bonded to Austin's blood. The side effect of this is that Austin and Jared are linked."

"There's no way Hornerstern knew this would happen," Austin said.

"Maybe not, and maybe he hasn't figured it out yet, but when he does you better believe he's going to use it against us."

Hannah collapsed onto the chair in front of the screen. They must have given Jared something to sedate him because after the orderlies returned and shot him up with something, he had collapsed. It had taken three of them to lift him and get him back onto the bed. Once they restrained him, they left the room. Tears streaked Hannah's face as she watched Jared lay there all alone. He had been there for her when she had needed him the most, and now the tables were turned, and she couldn't help him.

"Is there anything we can do to get his mind back?" She whispered.

"If there is, we'll find it," Nick vowed, as he walked over to her.

Nick knelt next to her and draped his arm around the back of the chair. His presence comforted her. Hannah felt like she was betraying Jared just sitting so close to Nick. Especially since she had been on the dance floor tangled up in Nick, while Jared had been getting captured. Even worse now, she wanted to sink into Nick's chest and let him hold her. She was just as torn for Nick, though. He was sitting next to her, ready to comfort her, and vowing to her that he would mend the man who was keeping her from him. That was something she would probably never be able to comprehend. Hannah didn't feel as if she deserved either of them.

"Nick, you can't let Austin and Jared fight. I can't lose anyone else. I won't."

"I know. We'll figure something out, Hannah. I promise."

"Thank you. I don't deserve you, but I'm so thankful for you."

Nick's face twisted with confusion as he looked at her.

"Hannah, it's me who doesn't deserve you. I'll do everything in my power for the rest of my life to try to make up for what I've put you through."

"Even bringing back the man who stands between us?"

"Jared doesn't stand between us. You chose him. Don't doubt yourself."

Hannah wiped a stream of tears from her face. She thought with time maybe her love for Nick would lessen, but it hadn't. The strength of her feelings for both men was still potent. Their harsh grip on her felt suffocating most days. She had never imagined she could love two men so completely, but it was as if she had two hearts; one for each of them. She turned back to Jared. Nick was right; she had chosen Jared, and she would fight until he was back at her side.

"We need to devise a plan to get Jared back," Nick said, standing and moving away from Hannah.

"First, we need to make sure him and Austin aren't going to kill each other. Then, we can get him out and bring him back," Adrian argued.

"No, we can't leave him in there. Who knows how long it'll take to find something to counterattack that drug. We need to get Jared back, and soon," Hannah said.

"Hannah, I'm sorry, but we risk everyone's safety if Austin and Jared go at it. Besides, Jared doesn't seem stable; if he would over power Austin—not saying he will but should he—and then he gets lose… There's no telling what he would do," Adrian defended his stance.

"Nick, please. We can't leave him there," Hannah sobbed.

"What if we just move Jared to another facility?" Nick suggested.

"Do you happen to have someplace that's equipped to hold a super human who's hell-bent on revenge?" Adrian scoffed.

"Actually…" Nick said, letting his sentence hang.

"You field agents have all the fun," Adrian chuckled.

Chapter Eleven

Nick

Austin and Nikki had been gone for a while to prepare the storage unit Nick had, for the arrival of Jared. Nick, Hannah, and Adrian had been studying Jared's behaviors and hatching a plan to get him out of Headquarters.

"I think it's best if we go in tonight. They won't be expecting us to just stroll up to Headquarters and take Jared," Adrian said.

"Jared will though," Nick countered.

"They've been keeping him sedated throughout the day. We wait until right after a round of sedation, so he won't be able to fight us."

Nick was nodding as he considered the plan. Watching what they were doing to Jared all day had been hard on Hannah. From what they had seen on the video feed, it was the only way. Jared just kept growing increasingly hostile. He was frantic to find Austin and kill him. Nick knew he had been the one to vow they'd bring Jared back, but he was afraid he was just setting Hannah up for more heartbreak. Adrian still hadn't found any information on something to counteract what Headquarters had done to Jared's mind. If the past few hours were any indication, it wasn't just going to wear off either.

"Maybe if I stay with him at the storage unit and talk to him, it'll help him remember."

"I don't think so, Hannah; he doesn't realize you are you, and he's very aggressive. If you claim to be Hannah, he may see you as a threat and attack you. We can't risk it. You will stay away from him until we figure something out."

"There is no information out there on reversing it. I'm no doctor, but this seems to be permanent."

"That's it," Nick said, as an idea sparked.

"What's it?" Hannah said, her eyes growing wide with hope.

"The doctor. We take him. If there's a way to fix what's been done to Jared, I'd say he's the only man who'll know."

"Awesome, so we're going to add kidnapping a doctor to our list of wrongdoings," Adrian said sarcastically.

"If someone's keeping track of mine, I'd say they'll think this is minor in comparison to the things I have done over my career," Nick replied.

Hannah's face fell after Nick's statement. There was no need to sugar coat the things he had done, but seeing it reflected there in her gaze made his stomach sink. He shook it off. The skills he had would be what would bring Jared back to her, and what had potentially saved people's lives. He could never regret the life he had chosen to live, just the fact that he had involved her.

"Once I take the doctor, we'll be working on a ticking clock. After Hornerstern figures out the doctor's missing, it'll only be a matter of time before he realizes I'm coming after Jared," Nick said, finalizing the plan out loud.

"Any developments?" Austin asked in lieu of a greeting, when him and Nikki returned.

"I'm taking the doctor. Is the storage room prepared?"

"As ready as it'll ever be," Austin replied, never missing a beat over Nick informing him he was kidnapping a doctor.

"Yeah. Adrian, you have a location?"

"Texting it to you now."

Austin turned to kiss Nikki goodbye, and the scene made Nick's heart clench. He'd never get used to not being able to grab Hannah and kiss her. As he approached her, he could see the anticipation in her eyes, but also the guilt. She felt it, too. She was fighting it as much as he was. Every time though, she chose Jared. Hannah chose not to give into her feelings with Nick, so he would respect that decision. He would forever be thankful for the night they spent together right after she discovered he was alive. It was selfish, but he didn't care.

"Be careful," she whispered.

"Always. Hannah, this doctor may be able to give us good news, but I also want you to be prepared for the worst," he warned her.

She nodded her agreement.

"I know. We have to try, though. I won't give up on him,"

Nick nodded and then turned to follow Austin out the door. His feelings were mixed. He didn't wish anything bad on Jared since he had been there to protect and care for Hannah when she needed someone the most; there was that selfish bastard in the back of his mind, though, telling him to let Jared stay in the darkness. Then Nick could have Hannah. No matter what he did, she would always be his end game.

Chapter Twelve

Hannah

Hannah and Nikki sat down on the couch in silence for a while; neither really knowing what to say. Adrian was still thoroughly engrossed in something on his laptop, so he wasn't much for entertainment. Not that either woman was in the mood to be entertained.

"I'm sorry you got dragged into all of this. It's pretty crazy, right?" Hannah said breaking the silence.

"It's a bit much. I'm not sure if it's the lack of sleep or just whatever this is going on between me and Austin is legitimate, but I just feel like this is where I'm supposed to be. I've never felt like I fit in, or I belonged; I was just existing."

"I think you two have something real. Austin hasn't shut up about you since we got in town. Sounds like he had been pursuing you for a while."

"We never really went anywhere, but he came into the diner every day. Sometimes he would stay after everyone else and keep me company while I closed up."

"That makes me happy. I've known Austin my whole life, and he's always been alone. I mean he has Nick and I, but never someone of his own. He needs that now more than ever."

Nikki smiled, her eyes going to that faraway place that Hannah knew all too well. Whether Nikki or Austin had admitted it yet, they were in love. It looked so easy from the outside looking in. When Hannah had fallen for Nick, it had been easy. They had been so young; they were too naïve to know any better. Life was getting them back now. Everything was complicated and going to hell in a handbag.

"I bet you're tired of all of this. Austin told me about everything that happened with Nick and you and Jared. I hope I'm not overstepping by bringing it up, but don't be so hard on yourself."

"I am. I'm tired of it all. Nick is, too. He's been through so much because of Hornerstern and his greed, and now Jared and Austin have been altered for life. I don't know what I'll do if we can't find a way to reverse Jared. He brought me so much light and happiness when it was absolutely vital for my survival."

"I know I haven't known you long, but was that why you chose him once you found out Nick was alive?"

Hannah opened her mouth to respond and then just as quickly shut it. No one had ever just come out and asked her why she had chosen Jared over Nick. If she were being honest with herself, she had never even asked herself that question.

"I'm so sorry. I shouldn't have asked you that; it was rude and inconsiderate," Nikki stammered.

"No, you're fine. I was just thinking how best to answer you. I suppose it's yes and no. Both men know I love them, and they seem to carry on just fine with the knowledge. I love them both differently, though. Nick is like this epic love that I've had for so long I don't really have a choice. He's ingrained in me. After I buried Nick, I lost it, and I never thought I would recover. That kind of love is petrifying to me now. Jared is light and carefree, and he's so easy to love. Our life together is easy, aside from this bit of craziness. I can be happy with him. I needed that kind of love in my life."

Hannah watched as Nikki digested what she had just said. She could tell by the look on Nikki's face she had something to say. Looking at Nikki was like looking in the mirror Hannah had been avoiding for the past few months.

"Spit it out," Hannah sighed, after a minute of avoiding the inevitable. "It's written all over your face. Everything I have been hiding from for months now is just staring back at me. I love Jared, but it'll never be the way I love Nick. I can't love Nick, though. He's so invested in all of this, and he feels so responsible; he'll never stop, and I just don't think I could handle burying him again. I couldn't. It would absolutely kill me."

"I can't imagine what you've been through, and I'm by far no love expert."

"But…" Hannah said, with a chuckle.

"*However,* people search their entire life for an epic, powerful, and yet petrifying, love. Some of them never find it. You have found it, and not only that, but you've gotten a second chance at it."

"Ugh. Nikki, I'm glad you're here, but that was a whole lot of truth I just don't think I'm ready to deal with just yet."

"Well if you ever get to the point where you're ready to deal with it, and you need an ear to listen or a shoulder to cry on, I'm here."

"Thank you. It's nice to have another female around for a change. For as long as I can remember it's just been me and the guys."

"I know what you mean. Not about being friends with just guys, but just about having a friend around. I feel closer to you all than I have to anyone else. That's pretty sad isn't it?"

"No, it's not. There are some people who are just meant to be in your life. I believe that now more than ever."

"Shit!" Adrian exclaimed, snapping the girls from their conversation.

"What's wrong?" Hannah asked, as she and Nikki stood and flanked Adrian's side to see what he was seeing on the computer screen.

"Let me guess, that guy's the doctor Austin and Nick just went to kidnap?" Nikki asked.

"You got it. The location I gave Austin and Nick may be a trap."

"What do we do?"

"Nothing. If there's any two people who can get themselves out of a pickle, it's those two."

"How far out should the guys be from the address you gave them?"

Adrian checked his watch.

"Any minute now."

Everyone was silent while they waited. The doctor was checking Jared's vitals and reading over the chart. Jared had been sedated for almost an hour. Hannah's heart clenched as she watched him. Even after the truths she had just spilled for Nikki, she still felt the rush of her love for Jared. The door to the room slowly opened. Hannah's heartbeat picked up. Jared stirred on the table. The doctor glanced at the door, but then back at Jared who had started shaking uncontrollably.

Nick and Austin stepped inside of the room and closed the door behind them. The scene looked casual enough, but Hannah knew tensions were rising.

"Is the volume turned up?"

Adrian checked it before nodding his confirmation.

"Doctor Walker?"

"Yes, and who are you?"

The doctor turned and took in the two agents, placing himself in front of Jared, protectively.

"We need to have a chat," Austin growled.

At the sound of Austin's voice, Jared sat straight up. He ripped at the monitors attached to him as he stood. Austin was rigid, and both men's eyes were glowing blue. No one in the room moved, but they were all ready to fight.

Jared lunged first. Hannah screamed as Jared went for Austin's throat. Austin deflected Jared's blow quickly and effortlessly, but his strength still sent Jared flying across the room. Jared jumped back up, even angrier, and went for him again. Austin fended off the punches and kicks that Jared was throwing like wild. Even though Jared had been injected with the same serum, his lack of experience with his skills made him no match for Austin.

Nick pushed the doctor back against the wall and took up a protective stance in front of him, looking unfazed. Occasionally, the fight would get close to Nick, and he would have to shove someone away from him and the doctor or offer a few blows of his own. Austin stayed on the defensive, but Hannah knew it was only a matter of time before Austin had to take the offense. He would have to do something so they could get out of there.

"This is taking too long. They need to get out of there," Adrian said, voicing out loud exactly what Hannah was thinking.

"I know. Austin's going to have to knock him out or something," Hannah winced at her statement.

"It'll be okay, Hannah. Once we get him back here, then we can work on helping him."

"I know."

Jared lunged to tackle Austin once more, but this time Austin wrapped Jared up quickly in a form of a headlock. Jared struggled and fought savagely, but Austin's strength and endurance was no match for him. Austin squeezed harder, and Jared went limp in his arms.

"Doctor, sedate this man. We need to take a little trip," Austin announced, propping Jared up against the bed.

The doctor was visibly shaken, but he moved about the room to do as he had been told. After they had Jared secure, Nick pulled a gun from the waistline of his pants and held it at the doctor's back.

"You're going to walk with us, and if you alert anyone along the way that there's anything wrong, I'll put a bullet in everyone you hold dear."

Hearing Nick's threat startled Hannah. It also reminded her that he was a man she didn't really know. She'd like to naively believe that Nick would never actually harm any one's family, especially after all she had been through, but she also knew there was a reason he was at the top of his career. Just like that, she slammed the door shut on her love for Nick.

Chapter Thirteen

Nick

After they had made it back to the hotel, Nick sought out Hannah. Her eyes searched his for answers. It was like a bullet to his heart. Gone was the glimmer of love. She had seen him for what he was: an agent. Always an agent.

"I think you should let me go to him," Hannah demanded.

Nick knew that Hannah was going to want to go to Jared. Nick also knew that hell would freeze over before he let her set foot in the room with Jared in the state he was in.

"Dammit Nick, quit ignoring me! I deserve to go in there and try. I can convince him, I know I can."

"Hannah, we do not know a damn thing about this drug that is messing with his mind. Sending you in there is suicide, and you're not someone I'm willing to risk. I don't care how much you hate me for it."

"But there are people you would risk? Just like you threatened the doctor's family. Would you have done it, Nick? After everything I've been through, would you have harmed him or his family?"

Nick took a step toward Hannah. Even after everything she had been through, the world was still black and white to her; good and bad. Nick was currently the bad. Hell, if he were honest, he was probably just as bad as he was good, but he truly believed he'd been bad for the right reasons.

"If it meant holding my promise to you, to bring back *your boyfriend*, I would have, yes."

Hannah's eyes widened with surprise for a moment, then they flashed with pain before she turned away from him. Nick had probably taken it too far, but it was done.

"Enough. Dr. Walker, you created this drug; what can we do to bring Jared back?" Austin said, ending the argument between Nick and Hannah.

"The drug spent very little time in the research and development stage. There's not a whole lot I can tell you that you haven't already gathered on your own."

"Why use it then?" Hannah yelled.

"Ma'am, it was never my intention to hurt anyone. I was simply carrying out orders."

"Whose orders? Isn't there some sort of code you follow being a doctor that says you can't use a drug that's not even been fully tested yet?"

"Things are *different* when you're working with the government," Dr. Walker defended himself.

"*For*. You're not working *with* anyone, you're working for the government," Austin snapped.

"Did you find anything in the research you did conduct that would lead you to believe it will wear off?" Nick asked, calling a halt to the argument that was getting them nowhere.

"No."

The room fell quiet as they all digested what that meant. Hannah's emotions flashed through her beautiful blue eyes; first anger, then sadness, and then defeat.

"For what it's worth, I'm sorry. This man is being bred for something great though."

"*Bred?*" Nick asked, intrigued by the doctor's choice of words.

"Yes, this unit does incredible things for our country. With the use of my drugs, Dr.

Hornerstern and his team will be virtually unstoppable."

"So, Dr. Hornerstern has more of this mind-altering drug at his disposal, as well as the serum that enhances humans?"

"Yes. The mind alterations won't always be used for such things like your friend."

"That son of a bitch," Adrian said, drawing everyone's attention.

"What is it?" Nick asked, moving toward Adrian and his laptop.

"Hornerstern's going to inject everyone in the unit with the serum. He's making his own army."

"What does he need an army for?"

"He's coming for us."

Chapter Fourteen

Hannah

Hannah had moved past grief on the car ride down to their new safe house; now she was furious. Jared had breathed life back into her when she had been suffocating. She clung to him and the safety of their love. Hannah couldn't lose him. Jared didn't deserve to spend his life under the rule of someone else's ministrations.

"Hannah, you can't save him. I know that's hard for you to cope with, but you have to trust me. If he sees you, he will try to kill you. You don't want to see him like this,"

It was Austin's turn to try and reason with Hannah. She ignored him as well. Austin kept reassuring her that she needed to wait; that she should trust him and Nick to save Jared. Hannah remembered the seriousness in Nick's eyes when he had told the doctor he would kill his family. Even though he had pushed her away, and they had decided not to be together, she couldn't help but second-guess Nick's intentions. Would he really save the man who she had found love with after him? Hannah tried to clear her mind; she was angry, heartbroken, and vengeful which was a dangerous combination.

"You guys won't give me the chance. You don't know any more about that drug than I do, yet you get to make all the decisions. What if I can help?" She yelled.

"Maybe I don't know any more than you do. What I do know is that it's not worth it to me to risk your life!" Nick roared.

"It's not yours to risk, Nick. It's mine, and I think Jared *is* worth risking my life for!"

Nick's eyes softened and then hardened again. Hannah wanted to falter. Her heart pounded painfully in her chest, knowing she was hurting Nick with her words. There was a difference in knowing what she felt for Jared and having her shove it in his face.

"I don't," he said, deadpan.

"Nick, we need to gear up and head back north," Austin said, switching the topic.

"Okay," Nick said, never taking his eyes off Hannah.

Hannah looked over to Austin. They hadn't been at the new safe house long, so she wasn't sure why they were leaving again so soon.

"Where are you going?"

"We're going back for the serum. Hornerstern cannot have those type of drugs at his disposal."

"Hasn't the damage already been done? He's already injecting other agents."

"Will he stop there, though?" Austin asked.

"You guys can't go back there; he'll be better prepared this time. My God, he's got an entire army of super agents, now," Hannah said.

Panic began to set in. She couldn't watch Nick walk out the door. It was selfish of her, but with Jared in an unknown state, she needed Nick close by to know he was safe.

"Austin's had way more time to perfect his skills. This is what I do, Hannah. We'll be fine."

Nick strode out of the room as Hannah deflated onto the couch. She lowered her head into her hands. Her life was a mess. It had been since the day Nick had walked out and never returned. Hornerstern had caused all the hurt and destruction. That one man was wrecking so many lives, and yet he still remained intact and seemingly untouchable. Hannah was tired of being the victim.

Nick came back into the room, dressed in all black. Hannah took him in. He was beautiful. She remembered the morning he had left, she had woken up before him. The moments had ticked by as Hannah had stared at his perfect profile. He had light freckles that covered his shoulders. She used to try to kiss all of them.

There was a darkness to him that she hadn't seen there that day. The darkness that surrounded him was the same darkness that surrounded their story now. It also breathed fire into the passion they had for each other. A passion she never shared with any other man, not even Jared.

"Be careful," she finally said.

"Adrian will remain here with you. The doctor is keeping Jared sedated, and there's a lock on the door that only I have a key for, so you won't be able to get in so don't bother asking," Nick said, his eyes boring into hers, demanding her obedience.

She nodded. Nikki came into the living room, and Austin wrapped her up in a hug as Hannah watched them enviously. Hannah was happy that Austin had Nikki. She was grateful that Austin had walked into that diner and found her. He needed her love as he struggled with his new life. Hannah envied them as she turned back to Nick. The man she loved; the man she couldn't have.

"Nick," she said, stopping him in his tracks as he headed for the door.

"Yes?"

"I'm going to kill Hornerstern."

Nick slowly turned around to look at her. His hazel eyes searching hers. Instead of shock, all she could see was love and affirmation in his eyes.

"I will make this right for you, Hannah. I will make sure that everything you've been through is avenged."

"He has done nothing but torture me and those I love. I can't stand it any longer; I won't hide out any longer while he just uses us like pawns."

Hannah and Nick continued to look at each other. Finally, Nick nodded.

"Tomorrow we'll start back with your Krav Maga training. I know you've been through a lot, Hannah, and it's all my fault. I would give up anything and everything if I could change this for you."

"I know, Nick," Hannah squeezed his hand and got up to go to bed.

She already felt better that she and Nick would start training again tomorrow. Austin and Nick turned and walked out the door.

"I don't know how you do it. Every time Austin leaves my sight, I feel like I may not ever see him again."

"For years, I didn't realize I was doing it. I spent a lot of time hating Nick for taking that from me, but I'm starting to wonder if he hadn't been right to keep me in the dark."

"The only thing worse than your mother being right, is when your significant other is," Nikki laughed, immediately lightening the mood.

"I trust that you won't ever tell him I said that," Hannah giggled.

"Your secret's safe with me."

"They'll be back. One thing I *do* know about those two men is that they're a hell of a pair. I saw them get into I don't know how many fights over the years, and they could never be beat. Nick's a hot head, and Austin's methodical; they work well together."

"How long until you try to find a way to get into the room with Jared?"

"What makes you think I'm going to try?"

"Because I would."

Nikki looked over at Hannah. Her face was serious, but it was laced with concern as well. Nikki had practically read Hannah's mind. She had planned on trying to get into the room with Jared. She figured it would be futile, but she wouldn't give up on Jared without trying.

"I don't know if we can necessarily get you in the room, but I have an idea. We just have to convince Adrian to help us."

"What is it?" Hannah asked, intrigued and excited.

"Well, if Adrian puts one of his laptops in the room with Jared, and you get on the other one…" Nikki said, letting the rest of her sentence hang.

"That's perfect! Nikki, thank you so much. You're brilliant!"

Hannah jumped up and took off to find Adrian. He was setting up shop in the back of the house in an office. She filled him in on Nikki's plan and then held her breath while she waited for Adrian to answer.

"I don't see why not. Nick and Austin just said you couldn't go into the room. They didn't say your voice couldn't be in the room. Let me get everything set up."

Hannah squealed with joy. Her hands shook as she tried to think about what she wanted to say. What *could* she say to Jared to make him remember her? Their time together had been short, but that didn't make her lose faith in the strength of their bond.

Chapter Fifteen

Nick

"How long do you think it'll be before Hannah's trying to convince Adrian to let her into that room?" Austin asked.

"I'd say within seconds of the door shutting behind us."

"You're right. How are you doing with that anyway?"

Nick rubbed his hand over his face. The last thing he wanted to do was deal with his feelings about Hannah and Jared, if he ever *could* deal with them properly. He also knew Austin was relentless. Part of being partners was knowing that your partner had their head screwed on straight. It could mean the difference in life or death.

"She chose Jared. She loves him, so I'll do anything I can to bring him back to her. Hannah doesn't deserve any of the shit I have brought on her."

"Did she choose Jared, or did you take yourself out of the game?"

"Damn, man. I don't know. Honestly, I'm not really sure I want to know."

"Can't say I blame you."

Nick's phone pinged, saving him from continuing the conversation with Austin.

"Adrian sent us over the layout of the new building Headquarters is using. He's pinpointed the area he believes they're holding the serum."

"How?"

"He says it has to be refrigerated, and this wing has the biggest pull of electricity."

"Techies, man. That shit blows my mind. You ready for a show down with Hornerstern?"

"I hope the bastard's there tonight, but I'd say he's at home; safe and sound. His time's coming though," Nick vowed.

"I heard what Hannah said to you before we left. You really going to let her mess with Hornerstern?"

"No, if I have it my way, she'll never be in the same room as him; *ever.*"

"Agreed."

They pulled onto the street a few blocks from Hornerstern's new hide out. Darkness had already fallen, giving them adequate coverage. They both checked their guns and took one final look at the layout Adrian had sent them before they got out of the truck.

Everything went smoothly on their way in. They didn't hit any agents until they got closer to the wing where the serum was stored. The first agent hadn't been injected. Nick easily took him out. As they encountered other agents, though, they began to go up against some that had been enhanced using the serum. They were wild and incapable, though. Austin's months of training made them easy work, even when he was outnumbered three to one.

"Damn, man," Nick said.

Austin shrugged, and they kept moving forward. Nick heard footsteps behind him and reacted quickly, flipping an agent over his shoulder and slamming him to the ground. He struck the butt of his gun against the man's forehead, taking him out. Austin kicked the door in, splintering the three locks meant to keep intruders out.

"Holy shit!" Austin muttered.

As they took in the room around them, they couldn't believe their eyes. There were multiple glass door refrigerators all full of what they could only assume was the serum.

"We should have brought a bag."

They both began searching through the room looking for something they could use to move the serum. Nick found a bucket, and Austin dumped out a trashcan. Then they went to work.

"Think this is all of it?" Austin asked.

"As much as I'd like to search the rest of the place, I have to hope this is it. Our time has to be running out. We need to move."

Austin nodded. They made their way out of the room and managed to exit the building without any other unwanted visitors. Nick breathed a sigh of relief once they were back in the truck and on their way back to the safe house. He had no qualms going up against the agents and, if necessary, killing them. What he didn't feel right about was killing men who had no idea what they were fighting for. The thoughts of any of them being under the influence of the mind alteration drug didn't sit right with Nick.

When they arrived back at the safe house, Hannah and Nikki were both awake. Nikki flung herself into Austin's arms, and they took off back toward the bedrooms. Austin nodded toward Nick to ensure he would handle the samples. Nick wanted to hate Austin for leaving him with the work, but he couldn't be mad. Austin had his back plenty of times while Nick snuck off to spend time with Hannah.

Looking back at Hannah, Nick could tell something was wrong. She seemed at odds with wanting to talk to him about the problem, so he just left it.

"Wanna give me a hand?" He asked.

"Sure. Are these… them?" She asked tentatively.

"Yes. Hopefully these serums never get into the wrong hands again."

"Whose hands are you going to put them in?"

Nick paused, realizing that they hadn't really thought about what they would do with the serums now that they had them. Austin had contacts in other agencies that they could utilize, but could those agencies be trusted? The serums had the capability to be used as weapons; especially the mind altercation drug. That type of power shouldn't belong to anyone. That was the problem with power: the weight of it could be intolerable; turning even the truest of men to darkness.

"Nick?" Hannah said, breaking Nick's train of thought.

"Sorry. I'm not sure, really. We have to find the right person to trust with them, and I'm not quite sure who that is just yet."

Hannah helped him place the small vials in the fridge, her demeanor quiet and thoughtful. Nick had learned quickly with Hannah that she would talk when she was ready. He had always hated it. If something was bugging her, he wanted to know immediately, so he could fix whatever the problem was. Hannah had always hated that about him. She used to tell him all the time she didn't want him to fix her problems for her. All she had really wanted was for him to just listen.

"I skyped with Jared," Hannah finally admitted when they got the last of the vials crammed into the fridge.

Nick sighed. Leave it to Hannah to find a loophole.

"Hannah…" He started, but she interrupted him.

"Stop, before you go any further; it was a bust. As much as it pains me to admit, you were also right about it not helping. Jared, *that* Jared, is deranged. The more I tried to convince him, the angrier he got. That stupid drug doesn't seem to be wearing off any time soon."

"I'm sorry, Hannah. I didn't want you to go through that."

She nodded as she plopped down on one of the kitchen chairs. Nick pulled one out and sat down next to her.

"I'm sorry I never used to listen to your problems." Nick blurted out.

Hannah smiled at him. Her hand reached out and covered his. Nick's heart beat fast at the connection. He wanted to grab her hand and pull her onto his lap but forced himself to sit still.

"You had good intentions, Nick. To be honest after you—well whatever you call it—I would have given anything to have you mansplain something to me just one more time."

"Mansplain?" Nick asked with a small laugh.

"It's when a man explains something to a woman, and he talks to her like she's an idiot."

"I never talked to you like you were an idiot!" He defended.

"Not intentionally."

"Not ever!" Nick was completely aghast at having Hannah think he had ever thought she was an idiot.

She smiled at him softly and then stood up. Nick followed her into the living room.

"Good night, Nick," she said, pausing briefly.

Nick instinctively leaned in to kiss her but then stopped himself. His lips were just a breath from hers when he stopped. Hannah's tongue darted out to lick her lips, painfully slow. Nick groaned and fisted his hands at his side. Before he thought better, he leaned away from her.

"Good night, Hannah."

Nick watched as Hannah walked down the hallway back to the bedrooms. He wanted to follow her and offer her more comfort, but it wasn't his place. Austin and Nikki hadn't emerged from their room. Adrian was holed up in his office doing whatever techies do. Nick should have been used to being alone after the year he had spent being 'dead,' but it felt different somehow.

He figured he should probably sleep at some point, but he knew he was too wired. He decided to try out the small weight room he had seen set up in the back of the house. After an hour, Nick finally felt exhaustion take over his body. He showered and found an empty room to crash in. It felt like he had no sooner fallen asleep when Adrian crashed through the bedroom door.

"Come on, it's Hannah!"

Nick shot out of bed, the sleep not truly lifting until he was halfway through the house following Adrian. Once he hit the living room, he saw Hannah in convulsions on the floor with a very worried Nikki and Austin kneeling over her.

"What happened? What's going on?" Nick yelled at them. He knelt next to Hannah trying to figure out how he could try to touch her without hurting her as she flopped around. He finally just reached under her and picked her up wedding style and sat her in his lap as he tried to calm her.

"She injected herself."

Nick about dropped Hannah as he jerked up at that statement.

"WHAT?"

"I heard her in the kitchen, and I just assumed she was getting a drink," Adrian said.

"Someone get the doctor!" Nick roared.

Nikki turned to take off down the hallway, and Austin stopped her.

"Like hell you're going anywhere near that room. I'll get the doctor; you stay here," Austin said.

Austin came right back with the doctor. Hannah's tremors had already started to subside.

"How much did she inject herself with?" The doctor asked, as he checked Hannah's pulse and pulled up her eyelids and began shining his small light in them.

"I don't know. We just found her like this. Where's the vial?" Adrian asked, looking around at everyone.

They all started frantically searching for the vial that Hannah had used. Nikki finally found it on the floor of the kitchen.

"Here it is," she called, rushing over to hand it to the doctor.

The doctor turned the small vial over in his hand several times before he spoke.

"The good news is she didn't inject herself with the human enhancement serum. The bad is that she injected herself with the mind alteration drug."

"Shit."

"How will her mind be altered?" Nikki asked.

"I'm not sure. The only times we have administered it, we have subjected the patients to, uh, certain tactics to persuade the mind altercation drug to perform a certain function. Such as with Jared; he was stimulated for hours prior in regard to the thoughts we wanted him to believe."

"Maybe since she wasn't subjected to anything, she won't actually have any side effects from the drug," Nikki said, optimistically.

Everyone looked to the doctor.

"I wish I knew. It looks like we'll find out soon enough. Her seizures have stopped. She'll need rest now."

Nick was still holding Hannah. He lay down on the couch and adjusted Hannah so that she was laid out on top of him; her head nestled on his chest. Hannah's body went lax with sleep. Nick stayed awake for a while listening to the steady rhythm of her heart.

"I'll be here, Nick, to monitor her. Get some sleep," The doctor said.

Nick tightened his hold around Hannah, not trusting anyone but himself with her protection. After a while, Nick couldn't help but drift off to sleep. For a while he could pretend she was asleep on his chest by choice, and that they were back to their old life and nothing had ever changed. For a while Nick could have his dream.

Chapter Sixteen

Hannah

Nick. Her body responded immediately to him. She was lying on top of him, his arms wrapped tightly around her. When she opened her eyes and looked down at him, it was as if she was back to the morning she had lost him. His features looked soft as the morning light floated in from the large windows on the other side of the room. His dark hair was ruffled from sleep, and his chest heaved with the steady succession of his breaths.

"It's always been you," she whispered to him, her voice hoarse.

Nick's eyes fluttered open and filled with relief.

"Thank God, Hannah. How do you feel?"

"I love you," Hannah replied.

"Easy, Hannah," Nick said, adjusting them so that he could sit up.

"What happened? Do you not love me anymore?" Hannah asked, a sob rising in her throat.

She was confused by Nick's standoffish reaction to her. They loved each other; wasn't that the way it was supposed to be? How long had she been out? Nick set Hannah down on the couch as he stood up and dragged his hand through his hair. He was shirtless with a pair of shorts on, giving her full access to his body. Her fingers reached out to trace the dark line of hair that ran down his well-defined stomach and disappeared into his shorts.

Nick stopped her by taking hold of her hand.

"Hannah, how are you feeling?" The doctor asked.

"I feel fine."

The doctor nodded as he listened to Hannah's heart.

She shoved his hands away and turned back to Nick.

"What's he doing?" She snapped.

"Hannah, you injected yourself with the mind alteration drug," Nick told her.

"That's impossible."

Hannah tried to focus on what she could remember last, but everything was a blur. Nick's death, followed by chaos, and then Austin becoming some sort of superhuman had all led up to them in the secret cabin in the middle of nowhere hiding out.

"Hannah, do you remember me?" Nikki asked.

"Of course, Nikki. You and Austin are together; see my mind isn't altered!" Hannah said a bit louder than she had intended.

"Is there anyone else you remember other than those of us in this room?" Austin asked her.

"Of course; there are lots of people in my life: my customers at the diner, my parents, Erika, and our dog, Presley," she replied exasperated.

"What about Jared?" Nick asked, his eyes searching hers intently.

Hannah thought hard. The name seemed to pull at something for her, but she couldn't recall ever knowing a Jared. She said his name out loud, but still nothing.

"I don't know any Jared. Is that a trick question?"

Nick looked at the doctor instead of responding to her. Hannah wanted to strangle him. She felt like everyone was talking in circles around her.

"It makes sense that the part of her mind that would be altered would have to do with Jared. That's probably the thing at the forefront of her mind, so it would have been the easiest for the drug to manipulate."

"Will she regain her memory back?"

"Unfortunately, there's really no way of knowing for sure. Jared's been under for a few days now and still shows no sign of regaining his real memories."

"Dammit," Nick cursed.

He stood up and ran his hand over his face while he paced across the hardwood floor. Hannah watched him intently, still trying to piece together what they were talking about. Apparently, her lack of knowledge of a man named Jared was big information.

Hannah found herself wanting to touch Nick again. It felt like it had been months since she had touched him. She tried to stand up but was hit with a wave of nausea. Nick rushed to her and helped her lay back down.

"You never answered my question," she whispered.

"Let's just take this day by day, for now," Nick said softly.

She didn't want to seem pathetic, but it felt like Nick was rejecting her. Hannah raged against herself trying to force the memories she was missing back, but nothing happened. The harder she strained, the more she couldn't seem to agree with the fact that she was missing any part of her past. It all led back to Nick. Whoever Jared was that they had asked her about wasn't in there at all.

How important could he have been, if she couldn't remember him?

Chapter Seventeen

Nick

Nick's heart swelled with relief when she woke up, but when she said told him she loved him, he thought for sure he was dreaming. He had never loved anybody or anything like he did Hannah. He knew he couldn't give into his urges to let the mind control drug give him what wasn't his to take. He had promised her that he would bring Jared back to her. The only thing that had changed now was that he had to bring her back to Jared as well.

Hannah wasn't in her right mind, so the words she was saying, even if she did mean them to some extent, were not hers. Nick knew that Hannah loved him, but she also loved Jared. If she were going to make a decision, Nick refused to allow it to be made under such circumstances.

He hated hurting her. Even though he understood what was going on, she didn't. Hannah thought he was rejecting her. His heart ached to give in and touch her. To pull her body up against his and feel the way it molded to him. Her body had been made for his.

"Austin, Nick, I have something," Adrian said, pulling Nick from his thoughts.

Nikki nodded to Nick and as he stood up to follow Austin and Adrian back to where he had set up his workstation, Nikki slid onto the couch next to Hannah. Nick didn't want to leave her, but Hornerstern would be preparing to retaliate. Nick checked the time, Hornerstern would no doubt be aware by now that they had taken the serums.

Nick and Austin followed Adrian back to where he had set up his office. Adrian punched a series of keys, and the screen came to life with a live feed back at Headquarters. Then Adrian turned up the volume so that they could listen.

"We need to find them," Hornerstern demanded.

"Everyone's still adjusting to the injections."

"Who is that?" Nick asked Adrian.

"That's Agent Brett Winland; he's fairly new, but he's good."

Nick nodded as they all continued to listen.

"There's a cabin in the outskirts of a small town just south of here in West Virginia. We've got a lead that they may be there."

Nick and Austin looked each other. If Hornerstern had tracked down Logan's cabin, there was a possibility that he had decent Intel from someone.

"Send me the coordinates. I can go in myself."

"You're no match for Agents McGraw and MacKenzie. Especially now that McGraw's not only injected, but he's had time to enhance his skills. You have no idea what you're capable of," Hornerstern scoffed.

The young agent's face contorted in disgust. He didn't like the bossman not having faith in him.

"Do they have any idea what they're even fighting for?" Austin questioned.

Nick just shook his head. Hornerstern had a way of leading people even if it wasn't for any cause at all besides his own greed. Nick wondered how many missions he had gone on that had been for that sole reason alone.

"Dr. Hornerstern?" Another agent came into the room.

"Yes."

"We have another agent that has come around."

"Who is it?"

"Agent Teegan."

"Shit," Austin said, his hand clenching in a fist.

Nick dragged his hand through his hair. Hornerstern had injected them all.

"We also have another one who failed to acclimate."

"Failed to acclimate?" Nick asked Adrian.

"Died."

"This is fucking crazy!" Nick bellowed.

"Alright, you know how to handle the situation. Please send me the appropriate details for his file," Hornerstern said.

After the other agent left, Hornerstern turned back to Agent Winland and studied him thoughtfully.

"I believe between you and Agent Teegan, you have a steady chance at gaining intel on the house in West Virginia. I'm sending over the coordinates now. Be ready to leave within the hour. I want you to go in under the cover of night."

The agent nodded and pulled out his phone and checked it confirming Hornerstern had sent him the information.

"Should we meet them?" Nick asked Austin.

"I don't want to kill those Agents," Austin said honestly.

"Adrian, do you know how many have failed to *acclimate*?"

"That's the fifth one. I'm not sure, but I think Hornerstern's having their deaths staged if they have families so that they can receive their benefits."

"How fucking thoughtful of him," Austin spat.

"These two agents, I know Teegan doesn't have a family, but what about the other one, Winland?"

Adrian began typing away on his laptop and then pulled back when he had an answer.

"Agent Winland doesn't have any beneficiaries listed on his paperwork."

"Let's go give them someone to find at that cabin," Austin said.

Chapter Eighteen

Jared

The only time he was at peace was when he was asleep. Sleep didn't come that easily now that the doctor was withholding the drugs from him. He begged for them, and the doctor refused. Then they tortured him with the sound of Hannah's voice, but it wasn't her. They were trying to pass some other woman off as Hannah to save their worthless lives.

Hannah was dead. Jared should have taken Hannah away when he had the chance. Before she had ever known Nick was alive; before Austin had the chance to kill her. Jared pulled at his restraints desperate to find Austin and kill him. He screamed out his anger and despair until his throat was raw.

The door opened and shut, indicating that the good doctor was back. Jared prayed the man was going to sedate him. He wanted to sleep, for the torment to end, even it was only for a little while. His dreams were always of Hannah and their time together. She haunted him.

"Jared. It's Doctor Walker, I'm going to give you something to help you sleep again."

"You can't keep me caged forever. Tell him that. I will get out of here, and I'm coming for him," Jared threatened while the doctor worked.

"Jared, Hannah is not dead. We've tried to convince you of this. Your mind has been altered to believe otherwise, but she is alive and in this very house."

"Do you really think I would fall for your lies. The woman you're trying to pass off as Hannah is nothing like her."

"Count backwards from ten, Jared," The doctor instructed as he injected him with the sweet bliss he craved.

Jared didn't bother counting out loud. As the drugs took hold of him, Hannah's face filled his mind. She was laughing, her beautiful blue eyes dancing with delight. Jared tried to reach out and touch them, but as usual he couldn't. Then her face began to fade, and instead the woman's face from the laptop came into view.

He struggled against the image. His Hannah popped back in his mind then, and he focused back in on her. The respite was short lived as the other woman's face snapped back into focus. The two images battled each other in his mind's eye. Jared realized then that even in his sleep, he would find no peace. The only way for him to be at peace was to kill Austin, and the woman pretending to be his Hannah.

Chapter Nineteen

Nick

Their trip back up to the cabin was quick. Nick and Austin parked the truck at a nearby well pad staging area and finished the rest of the trip on foot. Once they got close to the house, Austin was able to use his gifts to scan the area to make sure they had arrived first. Once the coast was clear, they let themselves into the cabin and waited.

They kept all the lights off hoping to draw the two agents inside where they could surprise them.

"They'll be stronger," Austin whispered to Nick.

Nick just shrugged. He knew the men would be enhanced, but he had spent his entire career going up against people everyone feared. That was what set Nick apart from the others; he refused to let the fear consume him. If he didn't take down the worst of the worst, then who would?

"What are you going to do about Hannah?"

That was a conversation Nick definitely didn't want to have. When Austin had remained quiet on the subject on the car ride up, Nick thought he was be in the clear. He dragged his hand through his hair as he tried to ignore his friend's questions.

"Ignore me all you want, but you're going to have to deal with this. She no longer remembers Jared; isn't that good news?"

Fuck yes, it was good news, but Nick couldn't let himself believe it would be that simple. The selfish asshole inside of him wanted to take her up on her advances and let the chips fall where they may; consequences be damned. The man he wanted to be for Hannah knew he owed it to her to bring her back to Jared and let her make her own decision.

"You're a hell of a lot better man than me. I'd let the bastard rot while I took the girl," Austin continued, not caring that Nick wasn't participating in the conversation out loud.

Nick knew his comment was bullshit, though. Austin wouldn't want to win a woman's heart by deceit any more than Nick did. If the effects of Hannah's injection ever did wear off, she would never forgive him. That wasn't a chance Nick was willing to take; he had let Hannah down too much. The woman deserved to be in charge of her life for once.

"We've got company," Austin said.

Austin stood up; the tension radiated from his body. Nick knew he was letting his enhancements take over. Nick readied himself as well, as the they heard the distinct sounds of the doorknob being tested. The agents had to be rookies to be so loud.

As they waited for the agents to pick the lock, Austin and Nick moved into position. They flanked the entrance to the living room, hidden in the darkness. The agents finally made it into the house. They moved slowly through the small kitchen. Nick readied himself to jump, but he caught Austin's gesture from across the opening signaling him to wait.

Nick wasn't sure why, but he held back as the agents moved in front of him. With the same enhancements as Austin, Nick was surprised they couldn't sense them. He saw one of them point up to the loft and signal the other one to go. Once they were split up, Nick looked back to Austin, who was giving him the go ahead to strike, since he was closer to the agent who stayed below.

Nick stepped out and grabbed the man from behind, wrapping his forearm around his neck. Up close, he saw that he was wrestling Agent Teegan. Teegan threw his head back to try and headbutt Nick, but Nick had already anticipated that move. Teegan then grabbed Nick's arm with both hands and freed himself from Nick's grasp. Teegan's grip was strong, his enhancements starting to surface. Nick stepped back just as Teegan spun around and threw a wide left hook, which Nick easily blocked.

Agent Winland launched himself over the handrail of the stairs and landed on his feet directly in front of Austin. Austin reached out and grabbed him by his neck, lifting him off the ground effortlessly. The agent struggled in Austin's tight grip, but finally managed to land a solid arm bar on Austin's forearm, causing Austin to release him.

Teegan lunged toward Nick, sending them both crashing to the ground. Nick knew he couldn't end up underneath of Teegan for long; with his newfound strength, it would be too easy for Teegan to overpower him. Nick threw his leg around Teegan's and used his momentum to flip them so that he had Teegan pinned to the ground. Teegan threw another punch, managing to the land it on Nick's jaw. The hit felt like it came from a sledgehammer, stunning Nick for a moment. Teegan took the opportunity to kick Nick off him. Before Teegan could pin him, Nick rolled to the side, sending Teegan sliding into Austin.

Austin managed to keep himself upright. He and Agent Winland were exchanging punches that neither of them seemed fazed by. Nick grabbed Teegan by the shirt and yanked him back to his feet and then slammed him against the wall. The agent still didn't seem fazed, so Nick threw a series of punches, landing them on the agents face and chest, hoping to throw him off. Nick was starting to feel winded, but Agent Teegan still looked fresh. He even smiled at Nick, which pissed him off.

Teegan pushed himself off the wall and advanced on Nick. Nick kicked him in the chest, then grabbed one of Teegan's arms, spinning him so that he could get him in a headlock again. Once he had Teegan in a headlock, he slipped into the sleeper hold. Nick held on tight as Teegan thrashed about trying to throw Nick off him. Finally, Nick felt Teegan's strength dwindle, and within minutes the agent collapsed on the floor.

Nick turned to help Austin, but Austin was just settling matters with his own opponent. Austin brought Agent Winland's head down just as he brought his knee up. The agent crumpled to the floor as well.

Nick dropped his hands down to his knees while he tried to catch his breath. It had been a while since he had an opponent who required that much strength to fight. He also hadn't been training regularly with all the craziness.

"You good?" Austin asked him.

"Yeah," he huffed.

"Hell of a fight."

Nick let out a chuckle when he saw the joy on Austin's face. The man had always loved a good fight, but he figured finding someone who could keep up now that he was enhanced had been a rush. Part of Nick wondered if he it wouldn't be worth it for him to get injected. Had there been more than two agents at the cabin, Nick wasn't sure if he could have kept up.

"Let's get them restrained. Once they wake up, we'll see if we can break them."

Chapter Twenty

Hannah

With Nick and Austin gone, Hannah was left alone at the house with nothing but her own thoughts. That, and Nikki's running dialogue. Hannah was grateful for the company, but the constant mention of the man named Jared was driving her crazy. She still didn't remember him, nor did she want to. She loved Nick. That was all there was to it. Adrian's phone rang from back in his office, which had Hannah and Nikki looking at each other. They hadn't heard back from the men since they had taken off, and both of them were anxious to know if they were okay.

A few minutes after the phone call, Adrian walked into the living room.

"They're fine; they probably won't be back today, though," with that Adrian disappeared again.

The doctor came out from the back of the house. Hannah's stomach turned because she was positive the doctor was going to push her to regain her memories of Jared.

"Hannah, how are you feeling?"

"I'm feeling fine."

"I'd like for you to come with me, please."

He didn't wait to hear Hannah's response, he simply turned on his heal and took off down the hall. Hannah wanted to remain where she was just to put the arrogant doctor in his place, but she knew it wouldn't get her anywhere. Everyone was hell bent on her remembering Jared, so she stood up and padded back through the house to where the doctor was.

The doctor had a computer with a video brought up on the screen, and there was the man who was tormenting her life.

"If he's just on the other side of the wall, why do we have to use a computer for us to communicate?"

"Because he's very dangerous right now."

"I was always told to stay away from dangerous men," Hannah said sarcastically.

"I know this is all very confusing, but with little information to go on for this drug, we need to figure out if there is a way to reverse the effects."

"Why? Is this man my husband, father, brother; anyone I should know?"

"No, he's none of those things."

"Then why does it matter? If he's dangerous and doesn't even remember me, why can't we just let it go?"

"Just bear with me, please."

"Fine. What do you want me to do?"

"Just try talking to him."

The doctor hit a few keys on his keyboard and then turned up the volume on the laptop, and the noise from the man's room filtered into theirs. Hannah didn't say anything for a while; she just watched him. He was attractive, but she still didn't have any flutters of recognition. The doctor cleared his throat, which caught the man's attention, and his dark eyes locked onto the computer screen. He walked over and sat down in front of his own screen, his eyes scouring over Hannah. There was no recognition on his part either, just anger and hate.

The doctor motioned toward the screen, and Hannah rolled her eyes.

"Hello, there," she said.

"Hello," he countered.

"Do you know who I am?"

"I know you're an imposter," his voice deadly.

"An imposter? What makes you think that?"

"They want me to believe you're Hannah, but I know better."

"Yeah, and why would I pretend to be Hannah?"

"To save their lives why else?"

"Whose lives?"

The man huffed as if she were trying to play him. Hannah was starting to get concerned.

"I'm not pretending to be Hannah; I am Hannah. I'm not sure how else I can prove this to you."

"Prove it to me? There's nothing you can do. I *know* you are not her."

"This is ridiculous," Hannah said, throwing her hands up in frustration.

"What if I showed you both this picture?" The doctor said, holding up his phone.

There on the screen was a picture of her kissing the man she was currently arguing with. Hannah leaned in to get a closer look. Her arms were wrapped around his neck, and even though her lips were firmly planted on his, she was smiling. Hannah didn't know much about things like photoshop, but she wasn't sure how someone would have been able to photoshop them and make it so realistic. She looked over at Jared, who was leaning into his own computer screen to study the picture. His face was contorted in pain. His eyes darted over to hers, and for a second, she thought she saw a flicker of recognition there.

"Does this look familiar to you?" She asked him.

His eyes kept bouncing back and forth between her and the picture.

"Hannah?" He questioned.

"Yes, I am Hannah, but I still don't understand why I'm looking at a picture of us kissing."

"You don't know who I am?" He asked, clearly struggling to keep his decorum.

"So, you agree that I am Hannah now?" She laughed.

When her eyes met his, what she saw petrified her. His eyes were filled with longing. He may not be completely convinced, but he was starting to remember who she was to him. It looked like she must have been incredibly important. Hannah looked back down at the picture, hoping her own recollection would be sparked but it wasn't. Her only thoughts were of Nick, and if he had seen the picture. Hannah couldn't imagine a life where she was kissing someone other than Nick. It was no wonder he had been so standoffish with her. Did they all want her to remember who Jared was, just so she could rehash her adultery? Having everyone know that she had been unfaithful to Nick made her sick. She already hated herself enough over it.

"Hannah, it's okay. It's not what you think it is." Jared said.

"Shut up! Did you know I was married when you…you…whatever this is?" She shouted.

"He was gone!" Jared countered.

"I don't understand. None of this makes sense. Wait; is that why you want to kill him? You're more than dangerous; you're a monster. I'm glad I don't remember who you are and what we did."

His face fell at her harsh words. The doctor put the picture down, his face remained clinical and uninvolved as if he hadn't just dropped a bomb on her life. She looked back at Jared; he had moved back from the screen and was on his knees. He looked tortured and unsure. His fingers dug through his thick, dark hair, while his dark brown eyes looked lost and broken. Hannah wanted to feel something other than hatred for the man, but she couldn't.

"Hannah, I'm sorry this has caused you pain. I had hoped it would spark your memory. It appears that I've made some progress with Jared, though, so if you'll excuse me…"

Hannah didn't have to be asked twice. She flew out of the room and ran to the front door and out of the house. The air was thick and humid, but it made Hannah feel better. Without Nick there, and the demons from her unknown past stalking her, the house was making her claustrophobic. She walked down to the stream that ran alongside the house and sat down. On either side of the stream was a bank of rocks, and the sound of the water rushing steadily over them was soothing. Hannah watched small minnows swim passed, as she tried not to think about the picture.

Minutes ticked by and the sun soon faded into the night, but the moon was bright enough that she stayed out there. The crickets and the frogs had joined her, and their melodies paired with the running stream soothed her into sleep.

"Hannah!" Nick's alarmed voice jolted her out of her slumber.

She sat up and stretched, looking around.

"Hannah!" He yelled again.

"I'm here!" She called back, though not very loud.

Hannah looked around, but she didn't see Nick right away. As she started up the hillside back to the house, he came around from the back.

"What the hell are you doing?" He yelled angrily.

"I came outside earlier for some fresh air and accidentally fell asleep. When did you get back?"

"Just now and found your room empty."

"I'm sorry. I didn't realize I couldn't leave the house."

"Not without someone with you, you can't. Which has me wondering what the fuck Adrian has been doing all day that he didn't realize you were gone."

"Don't be mad at him. I'm a grown woman. If I want to leave the house, I will."

"No, you definitely won't. Not right now; it's too dangerous. Anyone could have come along and grabbed you, and then what would I have done?"

"Relax, Nick. I'm fine; all is well."

Nick yanked his coat off and threw it around Hannah's shoulders and led her back up to the house in silence. Hannah wasn't sure if she should tell Nick about Jared remembering her, or not, so she kept quiet.

"I need to go shower; why don't you go to bed," he said, his voice finally softening.

"I could shower with you," she purred coyly.

"No."

"Okay."

Hannah gripped Nick's coat and headed back down the hallway to her bedroom. Before she got too far away, she stopped and turned back to Nick, who was watching her.

"I'm sorry about Jared. I don't know why I did what I did, but I regret it."

"Don't say that; you don't know what you're talking about," he said gruffly.

"I know I love you."

"I know, but you love him, too; you just don't remember."

Chapter Twenty-One

Nick

As the water cascaded over Nick's body, he couldn't help but replay Hannah's fallen face when he told her she couldn't shower with him. He grew hard at just the thought of having her naked and wet. Nick had been wrong over the past few months when he thought it was torture to watch Hannah be with Jared. Having her want him and having to turn her down was the worst kind of torture. He gripped his erection and slowly worked himself over as thoughts of Hannah flashed through his mind: the way her curves felt under his touch, her moans, the way her eyes would hood over when she was aroused. He pumped himself faster. Hannah used to never let him slow down once she was close to her own climax. If he tried to prolong it, she would rock her hips and dig her fingers into his back so that he would continue the rhythm for her. He wished it were her greediness pumping him faster now, instead of his hand. Nick grunted as he came all over the shower wall.

He was spent. It wasn't enough; Nick craved Hannah so much he wasn't sure he would be able to continue to turn her down. He finished his shower and then stepped out into the steamy bathroom. With his towel wrapped around his waist, he cleared off the mirror. He looked like hell. He and Austin had worked tirelessly on the two agents at the old cabin, but neither of them had given them any new information. No matter how hard Nick and Austin had tried, they couldn't convince either of them that they were fighting for Hornerstern's own power, and nothing more. Nick's vote had been to kill the agents, mostly because he was frustrated with not getting anywhere with them, but Austin had sent them back to Hornerstern a little more bruised and battered with a message. Austin wanted Hornerstern to know he was coming for him.

Nick slipped out of the bathroom and headed back to where the bedrooms were, but before he could get to his room, he heard Jared whisper his name from behind his locked door.

"Jared?" Nick asked, leaning close to the door.

"I remember," Jared said, his tone sounding more normal than it had since the injections.

"Everything?"

"Yes, the doctor showed me a picture today of me and Hannah and gradually it's all coming back to me."

"What about the effects of the enhancement serum?"

"Those are still there, it's just the mind alteration drug that's worn off. The doctor tried to wait up to speak with you and Austin about it, but he must have given up."

"I'm not letting you out of there," Nick said.

"I know. I just want to know what happened to Hannah. She doesn't remember me?" Jared's voice cracked, and Nick couldn't help but feel sorry for the son of a bitch.

"She thought she was injecting herself with the enhancement serum and instead she used the mind alteration. She ended up forgetting all about you."

"How fucking convenient."

"Look man, I don't want Hannah to have been injected with anything. I'd rather her choose for herself, *be* herself, as I would win on a technicality."

"What are you doing to fix it?"

"Nothing; the doctor didn't know if the effects would wear off or not. I wonder why yours did and hers didn't," Nick thought out loud.

"Maybe because mine's been in my system longer. I hope that means there's hope for Hannah's memory to return."

"I'm sure it does," Nick said.

As adamant as he had been for Hannah to regain her memories, he had also just got off thinking about her in the shower, so the thought of her going back to Jared made his blood boil.

"I'll talk to Austin tomorrow about letting you out, but we'll both have to speak to the doctor first."

"That's fine. I'm not sure I want to be out anyway."

Nick walked into his own room and slid a pair of briefs on while he thought about what Jared had said. Just a picture of him and Hannah today had done what they hadn't been able to reverse in the past few weeks of trying. Maybe Jared was right, and the effects had finally just worn off. Nick slipped into bed and tried to think of anything besides Hannah and what it would mean now that Jared's memories were back. Jared would be gunning for her. Here Nick was pushing her away, and Jared would no doubt be pulling her in. The odds were unfair though. Nick could just take her, and then when she got her memories back, she would no doubt be pissed he took advantage of the situation that way. He had to do what he thought would be best for her in the long run, even if it did kill him.

Exhaustion took over, and Nick fell asleep. His dreams of Hannah had been so real it was as if he could feel her body snuggled up against him. She smelled like vanilla, and her curls were tickling his face. Nick tried to roll over when the morning sun filtered into the room, but he was greeted by Hannah's warmth. He hadn't been dreaming. At some point during the night, she had crawled into bed, and he hadn't even noticed.

"Hannah," he whispered, nudging her awake.

She threw her leg over his and snuggled deeper against his chest. Nick's chest tightened as he fought for air. He was right where he wanted to be, but he knew it wasn't real. He couldn't let himself give in. Nick placed a small kiss on top of her head and then slid out from underneath of her. Hannah woke up then, her big eyes searching his for answers.

"Where are you going?"

"I need to speak with Austin and the doctor about Jared regaining his memories."

Her eyes fell away from his, and she looked defeated.

"Do you still not remember him?" Nick asked, sitting on the edge of the bed at her feet.

"I don't want to remember him, Nick. How could I have done something like that to you? How can you even speak to me knowing what I did?"

"I'm the one who should be wondering how you can still talk to me."

"You're rejecting me, though. I don't understand why we can't be together."

Nick felt gutted. He didn't know how to explain things to Hannah any better than he had been. If only they could figure out how to get her memories back. He wanted to fight for her, but on equal grounds.

"I'm not rejecting you, Hannah. I'm being cautious. I hope once this is all over with, you can look back at this and appreciate it for what it is."

Hannah sat up on the bed and moved closer to Nick. She was gorgeous in the morning. Her hair was a mess, and her eyes were always a deeper shade of blue. Nick longed to give into everything and throw caution to the wind. Hannah touched Nick's arm, and he felt his resolve soften. He needed to get away from her and put more clothes between them. Hannah had on nothing but a tank top and a pair of ridiculously short pajama shorts, and he was in nothing more than his briefs, which were stretching thanks to his growing erection.

When he started to stand up, Hannah tightened her grip on his arm.

"Kiss me, Nick. If you can kiss me and tell me that we're not real, then I'll stop trying."

Nick slid his hand around the back of Hannah's neck, letting his thumb rest on the steady throb of her pulse. He slowly pulled her toward him, knowing the whole time he was about to go down a path he wouldn't be able to come back from. His lips crashed against hers, and she frantically sought his tongue. She eased herself onto his lap, rocking her hips against him. Nick groaned, loving the feel of her in his arms. Their kiss was passionate and demanding. Nick placed his free hand on Hannah's ass, and then lifted her up so he could place her below him on the bed. He tore himself away from her long enough to take in how perfect she was all laid out on the bed, wanting him.

"I can't resist you, Hannah," he breathed, seconds before his mouth was back on hers.

Her legs wrapped around his waist as he covered her with his body. Hannah's hands explored his chest and back. Nick couldn't help driving his erection against her as his tongue mated with hers. Hannah arched into him, so he moved his kisses down her neck, sliding her tank top out of way to expose her breasts. She hissed with pleasure as he took one of her nipples into his mouth. He made love to both of them before he moved back up to take her mouth again. Hannah worked frantically to free his now throbbing member into her waiting hands. When she stroked it, Nick groaned, his body suddenly feeling almost too heavy for him to hold up. Hannah continued to work him while she whispered words of love and affection into his ear.

Nick was in a complete euphoric state. His mind became a frenzied mess of nothing but Hannah; touching her and feeling her. He pulled himself back onto his knees and yanked her shorts off.

"My God, woman," Nick groaned, when he saw that she didn't have anything on underneath of her shorts.

He slid his fingers down through her slick folds, marveling in how wet she was. Hannah slid her tank top up and over her head, leaving her completely naked and exposed to him. Her hips rolled under his touch, as she watched him from behind hooded eyes. Nick sank a finger inside of her, as his thumb flicked her sensitive nub. It had been too long since he had tasted her, so he dipped his head between her legs and replaced his thumb with his tongue. Hannah bucked against him and cried out his name. Nick licked at her like he was a dying man, and she was the only water left on Earth. Hannah's legs began to quake, and he felt her tighten around his fingers, before she crashed over into ecstasy.

Nick crawled back up her body, kissing her stomach, breasts, and neck before claiming her mouth again. Hannah's body writhed under him. Finally, Nick couldn't take it anymore, so he lined himself up with her entrance, and then filled her slowly.

"This is where you belong," she whispered into his ear.

He couldn't respond. He was lost to anything other than her and the pleasure of their union. He pulled out just to slam himself back down inside of her. Their rhythm was intoxicating, and Nick couldn't bring himself to stop or slow down. Hannah didn't seem to mind as she met his every thrust.

"Nick," she cried out as her body clenched around him, and she found her second release.

It was all Nick needed. He grabbed her hips and sunk inside of her one last time, as his own climax rippled through him. He dropped down on his elbows and leaned his head on her forehead as they both tried to catch their breath. She peppered his neck with kisses, until he finally rolled to his side. Hannah went with him and cuddled against his chest.

"I love you, Nick."

"I love you, too, Hannah."

Chapter Twenty-Two

Austin

"So, the picture just eradicated the drug?" Austin asked the doctor.

"I'm not sure it's quite that simple. I'm running tests now to check his blood work. I need to see if he has any traces of the mind alteration serum left in him before I say much more."

"How long will that take?"

"I have to send it out, so it'll take maybe a week."

"You can't just send it out. Let me know which laboratory you want to use, and I'll get the sample there for you," Austin said, narrowing his eyes at the doctor.

Even though the doctor was there and helping them didn't mean his loyalties weren't still with Hornerstern. Austin didn't trust the doctor to mail anything out or do much of anything except monitor Jared. Austin looked at his cell phone to check the time again. He wondered what had Nick occupied.

"What about the enhancement serum?" Austin asked.

"He says it's still intact. He's not as advanced as you are simply because he hasn't been allowed to train, but if you train him, he'll be just as deadly as you are."

"I don't know if I want him doing anything at this point. I want answers on that mind alteration drug before we move forward."

"What about letting him out of the room?"

"Only if he's accompanied by Nick or myself; otherwise he stays under lock and key.

Let me know the details on the lab. I'll be back."

Austin headed toward the kitchen to see if he could find Nick. When he rounded the corner, he almost collided with Nikki. He reacted fast and tugged her into his arms. She molded against him and tilted her head up to him, so he could taste her lips. Austin would never tire of having her near him. As long as he had lived thinking he'd never settle down, he couldn't fathom his life without Nikki in it.

"Good morning, beautiful," he purred when he finally ended their kiss.

"Good morning," she cooed in return.

"I'm looking for Nick; have you seen him?" Austin asked, still not letting Nikki out of his arms.

"I did; he was just in the kitchen. I think he went out on the front porch."

"Okay. Don't go far," he said with a wink.

She blushed as he released her and gave her a quick smack on the butt. Austin did find Nick out on the front porch. He was leaning on the handrail, his head hanging. Austin didn't have to get close to him to smell the sex.

"Well that answers the question of where you've been," Austin said with a sly smirk.

When Nick turned to look at him, Austin could see the pain in his friend's eyes.

"I fucked up," Nick said.

"Don't say that, man. You're in a shitty position. There is no right answer."

"I sure as hell know that Hannah's going to flip if her memory comes back, and she knows I took advantage of her."

"Is that what you think just happened between you two? That's fucked up, man. Whether Hannah is under a mind alteration drug or not, she loves you."

"Loving me and wanting to sleep with me after she clearly made her decision are entirely different things. I'm afraid she's going to hate me."

"She won't. It's Hannah; somehow the woman manages to love everyone around her despite all the ugly shit life keeps throwing at her. I'd say what happened between you two was inevitable."

"Jared remembers," Nick said, changing the subject.

"I know; I was just talking to the doctor. He's going to run some blood work on Jared. He wants to see if Jared still has any traces of the mind alteration drug in him. It could give us a benchmark to look for with Hannah."

Nick nodded.

"What's the next step with Hornerstern?" Nick continued.

"After our stint last night at the cabin, I don't think we can take on his army of super agents, even if we do have the element of surprise. We're going to need to pick them off one by one. I've been thinking about using the mind alteration drug to our advantage."

"No. I don't want anyone else losing a part of themselves because of this," Nick argued.

"If we know they'll get their memories back, what's the harm?"

"The harm? This, *all of this*, is harm. It's fucked up, and I'm sick of living in this world Hornerstern has created. No; no more mind alteration. I say we dump the vials down the sink."

"Nick, you're too emotional right now; think on it."

"I'm not emotional, Austin. I've lost my wife, only to get her back with a new man on her arm. Then I get her back again but only because she's not in control of her fucking mind. Now I'm dealing with this psycho turning men into super humans left and right, so they can come after me. To top it all off, I have to find a way to make the woman I love fall back in love with her new boyfriend. I'm done Austin. I'm done with the games. This shit is between me and Hornerstern, and that's how it's going to end."

Austin just nodded. He knew Nick had been through the ringer. It was all starting to get to him. Austin wasn't used to seeing Nick roused. He understood why he was, but it was concerning. If they were going to take down Hornerstern, he would need Nick at the top of his game, and as much as he hated to tell Nick, they were also going to need Jared.

"We need Jared," Austin finally said, after a few minutes of silence.

"I know," Nick growled.

"I'm allowing him out of his room as long as he accompanied by you or me. Otherwise he's to stay locked up."

Nick breathed in deep and then nodded his agreement. Regardless of what Nick felt, and the shit he was going through, he was an agent first. He would do what needed to be done, no matter what the costs.

Chapter Twenty-Three

Hornerstern

"They were waiting for you?" Hornerstern asked.

"Yes, sir."

"I don't think we have completely gotten rid of our mole then," he said, as he stood to pace his office.

"Sir?"

Hornerstern ignored the agent. He was less than pleased that they had come back not only empty handed but looking like the losers of the fight. The army he had created should be invincible, yet two of his men couldn't handle Austin and Nick. Had Hornerstern not been pissed about their failure, he would have gloated that they had proved his point: Austin and Nick had always been the right men for the job. He couldn't focus on that now, though. The tech agent who had escaped was weaseling his way around their systems. Hornerstern needed to lock it down.

"Bring me one of our remaining tech agents," he snapped at the men.

They rushed out to do his bidding. Mere minutes later, a techie he didn't recognize came into his office. Hornerstern took him in briefly before getting down to business.

"I want you to take this entire unit offline."

The techie's shock showed on his face. Hornerstern smirked, the man was definitely not a field agent with a poker face like that.

"Sir, that's not recommended. With servers down…"

Hornerstern didn't let the man finish.

"With our servers up, we are being hacked by one of our own. I need us shut down and locked up tight. I'll also need burner phones for every man in the unit, including myself."

"If there was a hack, I would know about it sir," the man said, trying to sound stern.

"Really? Have you checked the surveillance feed for intrusion lately?"

"No."

"Well had you done your damn job, then you would have caught our little hacker listening in to our plans to raid a cabin tonight. That hacker relayed the information to two very skilled agents who had they been tempted would have killed two of my newest assets."

The man looked around not knowing what to say. Hornerstern glared into him for a few more minutes knowing he was making him even antsier. Then he dismissed him to do his work. The events of the evening weren't a complete bust; at least now he knew Adrian still had access to their system. Once Hornerstern shut that down, Austin and Nick would be blind. A sudden thought came to Hornerstern, and he called the two agents back into his office.

"You said Agent McGraw was there, and he fought you?"

"Yes, sir."

"He overpowered you?"

"No, sir; he simply out maneuvered me. I had more strength."

Hornerstern flicked his wrist dismissively. Nick hadn't been injected yet. That was very interesting. Hornerstern figured once they knew he had a small army of super agents that they would have injected Nick. Hornerstern didn't care if he died trying, he was going to inject that man with the serum.

Chapter Twenty-Four

Hannah

Nick was going into the kitchen from the porch when Hannah stepped into the room. She wasn't sure why she blushed like a schoolgirl once their eyes locked, but she did. He enjoyed it, too. The corner of his lips turned up in a devilish smirk. Hannah tried to be nonchalant as she made her way to the coffee pot. Nick intercepted her, wrapping his arms around her waist and pulling her against him. Just as Hannah settled into Nick's hold, she felt him tense.

"You son of a bitch." Jared roared as he thrashed against Austin's hold trying to get to Nick.

Hannah was shoved behind Nick's back before she could react.

"Jared," Nick said, patiently.

"Fuck you! I knew you were putting your filthy hands on her! You're probably the one who injected her with the drug in the first place!"

Hannah tried to get around Nick, so she could defend herself, but he pressed her back against the counter firmly. Nick didn't say anything in his defense, though. He simply continued to shield her, while Jared continued to fight off Austin's hold.

"Outside," Nick finally said.

"Nick, you don't want to do this," Austin warned.

"Stay out of it, Austin. This is between Nick and me. It always has been."

"That's right; it has been, since the moment you touched my wife," Nick roared!

Hannah's heart sank at Nick's words. Even though she didn't remember Jared, or anything about their affair, she was mature enough to realize he hadn't been alone in it. If Nick was going to pummel him, then he needed to at least recognize Hannah's fault in the ordeal as well.

"Nick, this isn't all Jared's fault. I was apparently very much a part of the affair," Hannah said, grabbing Nick's arm as if she could keep him from moving.

"I want you to stay inside with Austin. Do not step foot outside for any reason," Nick commanded her.

"Like hell."

"Hannah, this isn't a negotiation."

"You're not going to take that man outside and beat him up because of something that wasn't entirely his fault. You've chosen to overlook my wrongdoings; he deserves the same. Whatever he is to you, it's not worth giving up over me."

Nick turned around, so he was facing her, and he cupped her face in his hands.

"You are worth everything. The only thing he is to me is a nuisance. This little quarrel we have here has little to do with you at the moment."

Austin still had a hold of Jared while the three men walked outside. Nikki grabbed Hannah before she could go outside too.

"This has been brewing; let them work it out. Men have a tendency to feel better after a few hits."

"I don't like this at all. Why did I do it?"

Nikki gave her a somber look and wrapped an arm around her shoulders. Hannah saw the men walk off the front porch through the far window. Moving closer to the window, she watched as Nick walked out into the yard. He was calm; his hands lax at his side. Jared was tense and coiled; anger rolled off him in waves. Hannah couldn't remember creating the storm that was unfolding right before her eyes, but it looked like it was about to unravel in the worst way possible. She held her breath as Jared threw the first hit.

Nick easily dodged the hit and returned his own, landing it in Jared's stomach. Jared didn't seem fazed by the hit at all as he threw another punch, nailing Nick in the chin. Nick's head whipped around as Hannah cried out. She pushed past Nikki and ran out onto the porch. Austin was waiting there at the gate, though, and he intercepted, her preventing her from going any further.

"Dammit, Austin; make them stop. It's not their fault," she yelled.

Austin didn't pay any attention to her as he tightened his hold. Jared tried to tackle Nick to the ground, but Nick was quick. He sidestepped Jared's advance, and Jared stumbled forward. Nick took the opportunity to wrap Jared up from the back, his arm locking tight around Jared's neck. Jared tried to turn in Nick's grip, his fists flailing about trying to land punches. Jared threw his weight back, and Nick went flying. Jared turned and pounced on him, locking him beneath him. Hannah fought harder against Austin's grip, anxious to get out there and stop the men from killing each other.

Jared had landed several hits on Nick's chest when Austin finally released Hannah, throwing her back, so he could make his way out to the fight. Hannah was hot on his heels. Austin grabbed Jared and flung him back with a flick of his wrists. Nick slowly stood up, shoving Austin out of his way, he went straight for Jared, punching him several times in the face. Before Jared could counter the attack, Austin got between them.

"Enough!" He yelled.

Hannah grabbed Nick's arm hoping to pull him back. The side of Nick's face was bruised, and Jared had blood pouring out of his nose. Jared turned to look directly at Hannah.

"I know you don't remember me right now, but I won't stop fighting for you."

She slowly shook her head at the man as tears began to gather in her eyes.

"I'm begging you to stop," she sobbed, and then turned and ran back into the house.

Chapter Twenty-Five

Jared

Jared felt like his heart had been ripped out as he watched Hannah walk away. He had to fight his initial reaction to chase after her. Nick started to follow her; Jared threw his arm out blocking his path. Nick grabbed Jared's arm and gripped it hard. The tension between them began to build again, but Jared didn't want to fight the man, so he struggled to suppress his anger.

"I just want what's best for Hannah," Jared said.

"She doesn't know what's best for her right now. I shouldn't have touched her, I know that, but I'll be damned if you're the one who dictates what I can and can't do."

"I get that. I just think ground rules may be best for our situation."

"If there are any rules to be made, Hannah deserves to be the one to make them."

Nick released Jared's arm and continued into the house. Jared looked around for something to punch. Austin was standing behind him with his arms crossed, a knowing look on his face.

"I don't suggest punching me; I hit back," Austin said, with a smirk.

"This is just so damn frustrating."

"I imagine so, but Nick's right; Hannah deserves to make the rules."

"How can she do that if she doesn't remember me? She's probably going say she doesn't want me anywhere near her or some stupid shit."

Austin just shrugged which made Jared angrier.

"What are you guys doing about Hornerstern?" Jared asked, hoping the change in subject would help cool his rage.

"I'm glad you asked. We're going to need your help. Nick and I met with two of the agents who have recently been injected. They were hiding in wait for us at the cabin. Nick took on one of them, and he struggled to win the fight. I can easily handle one, but if our numbers are correct, Hornerstern has at least ten super agents. Even with you trained, and on our side, I don't think we can take on those kind of numbers and win."

"Inject Nick."

"I get the feeling he doesn't want to do that."

"Tough shit. I didn't want to be injected either, but here I am. With the three of us, surely we can manage to take down Hornerstern's lackies."

"I still don't like those odds."

"What about Adrian?"

"He's never been a field agent; he's just a techie."

"Desperate times call for desperate measures. I'm not sure why we're waiting around for them to find us and catch us with our pants down. Inject Nick and Adrian, and that gives us better odds."

"I had thought of using the mind alteration drug to our benefit, too," Austin said.

"How so?"

"We pick off some of Hornerstern's boys and inject them with the mind alteration drug to turn them against him."

"I like it," Jared nodded.

"Nick doesn't."

"Is Nick running the show? I don't think this is just up to him. We're all here; we're all affected by this bullshit now, so we should all have a say on how this plays out. I like to win, so if that means we have to use chemical warfare to do so, let's do it."

"You may be right about one thing: we're all affected by this, so let's see what everyone has to say."

Austin turned to head inside. When Jared didn't immediately follow him, he stopped and waited. Jared huffed in agitation and then followed Austin inside. Nikki latched onto Austin as soon as he was in the door, which made Jared feel a pang of longing for Hannah. Adrian walked into the kitchen looking annoyed.

"What's wrong with you?"

"They blocked me. We are no longer able to access anything at Headquarters. We're blind."

"Shit."

"We should have known that was going to happen when we surprised those two agents last night," Nick said calmly.

"I kind of hoped Hornerstern would have chalked it up to instinct," Austin said.

"We need to make a move, and we need to make it fast," Jared said, mostly because he was itching for a fight.

"And do what? Take on the entire group of them? You've barely been in touch with reality, so I hardly doubt you're the one to make any of the decisions," Nick growled.

"Maybe not, but we're all affected by this; it's not just you Nick, so we should make the decision as a group."

Nick held Austin's gaze for a bit, an unspoken conversation obviously passing between the two men. It annoyed Jared. He had every right to be a part of the conversation. Hell, he felt as if he had more at stake than Austin or Jared. He had been injected against his will with not only the enhancement serum but a mind alteration drug as well. He was currently without Hannah thanks to the mind alteration drug and would be until hers wore off, *if* it wore off.

"I'm with Nick, I don't think you all need to go anywhere," Hannah's small voice said, from behind Nick.

Nick moved to the side, so she could be a part of the conversation. Her eyes were still wet from her tears, but she avoided looking at Jared. He silently recited a prayer that her eyes would land on his, but with recognition instead of anger and distance.

"I have to agree with them. We're blind right now, and that's dangerous; especially since we're out numbered," Adrian added.

"What if you inject yourself?" Jared asked.

"I'd be of no use in a fist fight with or without the enhancement serum."

"How do you know? The enhancement serum doesn't just make you faster and stronger; it'll make you a fighter. It'll be ingrained in you," Jared countered.

Adrian's eyes hardened on Jared.

"Let's all just think on our options and reconvene tomorrow."

Chapter Twenty-Six

Hannah

Their time at the safe house seemed to tick by effortlessly. It had been two weeks since Jared had realized Hannah wasn't dead, but Hannah still had no idea who the man was to her; other than the man she had cheated on Nick with. Even though Nick had spent every night in the same bed as Hannah, he hadn't made love to her again. She knew it was because of all the unknown crap between her and Jared, which just infuriated her.

Jared didn't seem the least bit deterred by her constant efforts to avoid and ignore him. He was constantly trying to remind her of their time together. None of it ever worked. All it did was make her sick to her stomach to hear about it. A part of her did feel bad for Jared because he was clearly heartbroken. The pain was written all over his face, but Hannah couldn't let herself worry about him. Nick was the one who deserved her time and attention.

Any time he wasn't with Austin training or working out a plan of attack, Hannah would seek him out. Hannah had been trying to get Nick alone for most of the day since the men were all leaving at dark to go and stake out Headquarters again. Since Adrian lost his connection to Headquarters, they had all been scrambling, and tension was high. Hannah wasn't sure what they were going to do once they were there, but she hoped it would work. She was ready for the nightmare to be over.

"Hey, Hannah." Nikki called as she walked out to join Hannah on the front porch.

"Hey."

"Do you know any more about tonight?"

"I don't think so; just that they're going at dark. You?"

"That's the extent of my knowledge, too."

Hannah let out a frustrated sigh. She had hoped maybe Austin would have confided in Nikki. The men were out in the front yard sparring. Nick was shirtless, and sweat was rolling down his body, which made Hannah's womanhood hum in appreciation. For being the only man without enhancements, he was keeping up well with Austin and Jared, which made Hannah prickle with pride. Nick had always had an unbelievable strength. His parents used to tell her stories of his feats of strength even when he had been little. He was incredible to watch. It was always petrifying because Hannah knew Nick had to be strong, he had to be fast, he had to be at the top of his game at all times, or he could end up dead. Especially going into any type of altercation with Hornerstern and his new army.

The men all decided to take a break, and Hannah was thankful for the reprieve. Her nerves were getting the best of her. Austin strolled up on the porch and immediately tugged Nikki into his arms. The two of them giggled as Nikki tried to shy away from Austin's sweaty body while he tried to pepper her face with kisses. Hannah was jealous of the easy nature of their relationship. She could remember a time when she had been so carefree with Nick. Now as Nick walked up onto the porch, even though his eyes were locked on her, he never reached out to touch her. Just behind Nick was the reason why: Jared. Jared watched Hannah, too, and he watched Nick as if to make sure Nick didn't do anything Jared didn't approve of.

Hannah stood up a little taller and stepped into Nick's body when he cleared the top step. Nick's arm instinctively wrapped around Hannah's waist, which made her heart squeeze at how good it felt to have him hold her. Jared's eyes turned deadly, but he continued into the house.

"I think men are supposed to be the ones involved in the pissing contests," Nick whispered against her ear.

"I'm so sick of him dictating how you treat me."

"He doesn't dictate anything."

"Oh really? Since he remembered me, you haven't touched me at all. I'm constantly throwing myself at you, and you do nothing. Don't you want me anymore? Don't you love me?"

The door shut behind Austin and Nikki, but Hannah never took her eyes off Nick.

"I don't touch you because you don't know what you're doing right now; not fully. As for the rest, of course I want you, and I'll love you until the day I die; maybe even after that. I'm doing my best to hold it together the way I think you would want me to."

"I'm telling you I don't want you to hold *anything* together. Please, touch me, love me. I want *you,* Nick."

Nick pulled his arm from around Hannah's waist and began to pace the porch. Hannah wanted to scream at him. He was tearing her heart out with every second of silence that passed between them. When his eyes met hers, she saw his resolve and threw herself into his arms. Nick captured her mouth in a passionate kiss. Hannah moaned against his mouth as his tongue swept inside her mouth to mate with hers. Nick was an amazing kisser but having him kiss her after what felt like forever of him refusing to, made it that much better. When Nick finally pulled back, Hannah was filled with lust.

Hannah was shocked when Nick stormed off the porch. She followed him and finally caught up long enough to grab his arm.

"Dammit Hannah, I need you to remember Jared, so you can make this choice yourself."

"I don't understand! I made my choice: it's you."

"It wasn't!" Nick roared.

Hannah's hand flew to her mouth as she took in the heart-breaking expression on Nick's face. She reached out to touch his hand, but he moved back.

"Before your mind was altered, you chose him. You didn't have an affair, Hannah; I was dead for all you knew. You moved on, with him, and when I came barging back in your life, you chose Jared."

Hannah shook her head. There was no way she had picked Jared. She wasn't sure why Nick was telling her these lies, but she refused to believe them.

"Hannah, it's true. Please baby, please remember. I want nothing more than to strip you bare and taste your flesh one more time, but I feel like I'm going against your wishes. I don't want you to hate me when you do remember."

"I won't hate you. I love you, and if I do remember Jared, I know I'll still pick you. I don't know why you're doing this to me, Nick, but I'm not giving up."

Nick cupped her face in his hands.

"I love you, Hannah."

With that, he turned and stalked off. Hannah wanted to follow him and demand more from him, but she knew it was futile. Nick had made up his mind, and if she was going to win him back, she was going to have to remember the man who was standing between them. Hannah turned back to the house and stormed inside where Jared was sitting at the table.

"Trouble in paradise?" He snarked.

"I don't know who you are or why you're doing this, but if remembering you is how I fix my marriage, then I'm going to remember."

She saw a brief flash of excitement cross his eyes, but then just as quickly they went back to irritated.

"So how did we meet?"

"I was assigned to protect you after Presley had been attacked, and Nick thought you were in danger."

"So, you knew Nick was alive when we met?"

"No, I was given my orders from Hornerstern."

"It's a bit unprofessional for a bodyguard to fall in love with the person he's protecting."

"I'm not a bodyguard, and yes, it is. I didn't want to fall for you, it just happened."

"Who made the first move?"

"It was mutual."

"Mutual? How is that?"

"You were wearing my shirt after you came out of the shower, and I wanted you bad that night. I went and took a cold shower to try and keep my hands off you, but it didn't work. As soon as I walked out of the bathroom our eyes locked, and you moved toward me as fast as I was going to you."

"Did you know Nick was alive when this happened?"

"I had a feeling, but it wasn't confirmed until the following day."

Silence throbbed between them. Hannah dropped down onto one of the chairs across from Jared as she processed the information. Nothing was giving her a flicker of memory though. Mostly, it was just making her sick to her stomach.

"Okay, last question: Why did I choose you?"

Chapter Twenty-Seven

Jared

The question echoed in Jared's mind. He opened his mouth to respond, but as he played back his time with Hannah, he realized he wasn't sure why she had chosen him. After several minutes of silence, her eyes narrowed at him as if she was calling him out on a lie.

"You never told me why," he finally responded.

"I walk away from the man I've been with the majority of my life to be with you after a few months, and I don't have a reason why?" She scoffed.

"It wasn't that simple. There were reasons."

"I'd like to know those reasons. They are very important to me."

"I guess I don't have the answer for you," Jared realized he didn't have the answer for himself either. Maybe it was something he needed to hear, too.

"Maybe I'll remember you tomorrow and all the reasons I chose you, but for now I haven't the slightest idea who you are or why I would have picked you. I'm sorry, Jared, but I'm begging you to please let me be happy. Let me move on."

Jared remembered a sign that his grandma had hung up on her wall that read, 'If you love something, set it free; if it comes back, it's yours. If doesn't, then it never was.' That seemed to resonate with Jared and his current situation. Maybe Hannah was his, and this was a test of some sort that he needed to pass. He had remembered eventually, so he could only hope that she would one day remember, too. Until that day, he would give her the happiness she was asking for. Nick had stepped back and let Jared fill that void, so it was only fair that Jared do the same now.

"I'm sorry, Hannah. You're right. If being with Nick now is what you want, and what will make you happy, then that is what I want for you."

"Thank you," her face broke out into a huge smile, and for the first time since he had been taken his heart felt whole.

Jared understood now why Nick had stepped back before. He offered what he could of a smile in return and then stood up and headed outside to find Nick. He finally caught up to Nick sitting down by the creek that ran in front of the house. It was a peaceful sound: the way the water slid over the smooth rocks and splashed against the creek bank. Jared sat down next to Nick, and neither of them said a word for a while. They weren't friends, but they also weren't enemies. There was a sort of quiet camaraderie between them, with Hannah being the holding anchor.

"Hannah never told me why she chose me," Jared finally said.

Nick still didn't look at Jared, nor did he offer any commentary.

"She asked me why she chose me, and I didn't have an answer for her."

Silence again followed his statement.

"That day at my house when I asked everyone over so I could tell you that I thought Hornerstern was behind it all; I asked Hannah to pick me that day. I told her I *needed* her to choose me," Nick admitted, without a single flash of shame in his gaze.

Jared waited for him to gather his thoughts and continue his story. Maybe Jared should have felt angry over what Nick had just admitted, but he wasn't. In a way, he felt bad for the guy, because Hannah had left with Jared that day.

"This is my life. I created this entire fucking situation. There are so many ghosts in my closet, that it's probably not a question of *will* someone come after me next, but *who*. Hannah knew that. She also knew that I wouldn't stop until Hornerstern was brought down, and I won't. I don't care what that means; I will see that man in the ground. That doesn't mean I don't love that woman with every single fiber of my being, though. I can't say that I feel guilty that she's with me right now, but I will admit that I'm terrified. Terrified that she's going to look at me one day, and I'm going to see the memories there in her eyes; the memories of you and her and all those reasons she walked out that door that day with you."

There wasn't anything Jared could say to the truths that Nick had just laid out. All he could do was continue to battle alongside his brother in arms. They were at war, but not really with each other, mostly just with time. When Hannah regained her memories that would be their judgment day. Jared decided then, that no matter what her choice would be that day, he would honor it and embrace it.

"I'd like to hate you, but I still don't know if I do."

"It's a real bitch isn't it?"

Chapter Twenty-Eight

Hannah

In the days following the fight between Jared and Nick, things actually began to calm down. Jared wasn't hostile, and Nick had given into Hannah. The men still trained every day, and Adrian still worked toward getting them access to Headquarters, but with no imminent threats, all they could do was wait.

"Wanna go for a hike with me?" Nick asked Hannah.

"I'd love to."

Hannah slipped on her shoes and followed Nick to a trail behind the house. One thing about their time spent at the safe house was Hannah was falling in love with the quaint home a little more every day. She had never really lived way out in the country before, and she always assumed she would hate it. For whatever reason, though, she couldn't imagine going back to her home with the busy street in front of it and the constant thrum of traffic.

"I love it out here. I know the circumstances are shit, but it really is a beautiful place."

"It is. Wait til you see where I'm going to take you."

They hiked mostly in silence, but occasionally Nick would stop to tell Hannah something about a plant or flower. Hannah felt like she was seeing a whole other side to a man she thought she knew everything about. Nick apparently had spent an ample amount of time in the woods for his *actual* job, so he had taken to learning about the things around him.

"Was there ever any other choice for you, as far as becoming an agent?" Hannah asked as they walked.

Nick seemed to think for a minute before he responded. "No. I'm sorry for what it's done to you—to us—but there's really never been any other way for me."

"I see it now. Had you asked me before all this mess started, I wouldn't have pictured you as an *agent*, but now that I know, I feel like I can really see you for who you are."

Nick didn't respond; he just grabbed her hand as silence fell between them once again. They hiked for roughly an hour before Nick finally told her they were almost there. Hannah was a runner, but the climb over the last hill was slowly doing her in.

"Here we are," Nick said, moving a tree limb to the side so Hannah could get around it.

The scene that opened up before her took her breath away. She felt like she could see for miles. There was a rock, in the shape of a couch, perched close to the edge, which made for the perfect viewing point. She and Nick took a seat and took in the scenery. Rolling mountains fell into one another, set against the beautiful cloud free sky. Hannah felt peaceful. Nick wrapped his arm around her, pulling her into his side.

"Thank you for bringing me here. It's beautiful."

"I hope you know that nothing is as precious to me as our time together."

"You act as if I'm going somewhere."

"I've learned to never assume anything."

"That seems pessimistic. I have to believe that you and I will always have a connection to one another; somehow we'll always be together."

Nick cupped her face and captured her lips in a kiss. It was a slow, passionate kiss that made Hannah's heart squeeze with her overwhelming emotions. When he finally pulled back, she was breathless. They snuggled against each other and enjoyed their haven for a little while. The walk back to the house was a little easier since it was mostly downhill, but by the time they got back to the house, Hannah was starving.

"Let's order pizza," Hannah said.

"You're addicted to that stuff," Nick laughed.

"It's amazing; please," she begged.

"Fine, but I want a meatball sub. I'm about pizza'd out."

"How is that even a thing?" Hannah scoffed.

"When you insist or ordering the Pizza Station every other day, the rest of us have had enough."

"Whatever," Hannah said, completely unfazed as she grabbed the phone to make the call.

"The line's dead." she said, turning to Nick.

He rushed over and took the receiver from her hand, listening for himself.

"Adrian!" Nick bellowed.

Adrian scrambled out of his office in the back of the house. "What's up?"

"What are you doing to the phone lines?"

"Nothing, why?"

Nick handed the phone receiver over to Adrian who in turned listen as well.

"Where's everyone else?"

"In their rooms I guess," Adrian said with a shrug.

Nick took off to the back of the house. Hannah wasn't sure what to do, so she waited for Nick to return. Adrian took off back to his office. Minutes later everyone filtered into the living room. Jared's eyes briefly landed on Hannah, but then just as quickly moved away. Hannah felt a quick pang of guilt for the man, but she too diverted her eyes back to Nick.

"Have you guys been in the house all day?" Nick asked.

Everyone nodded.

"I think it's safe to assume our lines were tampered with which means Hornerstern could very well know where we are."

"Why cut the phone lines though? That kind of gives him away, doesn't it?" Hannah asked.

"I'm not sure why he would show his hand, but it could very well just be a heads up that he's found us."

"Do we move on?" Nikki asked.

"No, we stay. I'm done running. If Hornerstern wants a fight, that's what he'll get." Nick said. The other men nodding their agreement.

"Are you sure we're ready? If we've been training, you know they have as well, and they have more enhanced agents." Jared commented.

"I believe we can handle this," Nick said, looking to Austin for confirmation.

"I think if Hornerstern has found us, let him come to us," Austin said.

"So much for freaking pizza," Hannah muttered.

Chapter Twenty-Nine

Nick

"Did you hear that?" Jared said, standing up.

Austin stood up too, pushing Nikki toward the center of the room. Nick couldn't hear anything, but he did the same with Hannah. Everyone stayed quiet while Jared and Austin listened. Adrian quietly entered the room.

"We have company," he whispered, holding up his Glock.

"Hannah and Nikki, get in the hall closet and stay there until one of us comes for you," Nick said.

"They'll be able to find them no matter what we do with them, Nick," Austin said, pulling a gun out of his ankle strap and handing it to Nikki.

"I don't know how to use one," Nikki replied, shaking her head, and holding her hands up.

"Fuck," Nick cursed as he handed Hannah her Judge.

Hannah shook her head.

"This is kill or be killed, Hannah. Can you do this?"

"Nikki, stay with Hannah," Austin ordered.

"Where's the doctor?" Adrian asked.

"He can fend for himself. Besides if we can keep the fight away from the house, it's a nonissue."

Hannah took the gun, but she grabbed Nick's hand as well and squeezed hard. He knew she was afraid, not just for her but for him and the others. Nick had hoped to get the jump on Hornerstern instead of the other way around. He didn't want Hannah anywhere near the fighting, but there was no time. All he could do was arm her and try to make sure no one got into the house.

"It'll be easier if we get them in the house. If we confine them they won't be able to double up on you." Austin said, as if he was reading Nick's mind.

"I don't want them that close to Hannah and Nikki," Nick voiced.

"We have to move guys; we can't talk about this any longer," Jared said, the need to fight reverberating off him.

Nick felt it, too. That age-old hum of adrenaline before confrontation. He could still remember the first time he had felt it when he had been in middle school and socked a kid in the teeth for making fun of him. The kid's tooth had come through his lip, and Nick had earned himself detention for a week.

"I still say we take the fight away from the girls," Nick argued one last time.

"You guys better hurry; they're almost to the edge of the wood line."

Nick grabbed Hannah and kissed her hard on the lips. Then before he left to follow the rest of the guys outside, he kissed her on the forehead; their longstanding tradition. She gave him a nervous smile.

"Come back," she mouthed.

He nodded before turning to leave. Nick had continuously refused to be injected with the enhancement serum no matter how many times he would get his ass kicked during their sparring sessions, but as the silence greeted him outside, he had a brief pang of regret. Austin and Jared had heard the approach from in the house, Nick still didn't hear anything, and he knew their opponents were close. He pushed his doubts and regrets down; he knew they would get him killed. Hannah had told him to come back, and he would be damned if he let her down again.

Austin stopped, and everyone else followed suit. Nick scanned the wood line, still not hearing or seeing anything. Beside him, he could feel Adrian's nervousness. The poor guy was a desk jockey; he had never intended on being out in the field, but desperate times called for desperate measures. They had taught him all they could about hand to hand combat in the past few weeks. He was also armed with a knife and a gun, to help give him an advantage. Nick didn't like the thought of killing men he had once considered brothers, but Hornerstern had left them no choice.

Just as Nick was about to ask Austin what the hell was going on, men emerged from the woods. There was no time to think after that, only fight. Nick had to try and keep his back toward the giant rock that was in the backyard. He had trained that way with Austin and Jared every day. If one of the enhanced agents were to get him from behind, Nick wouldn't be able to defend himself. His first opponent was strong and quick, but he didn't have any instincts. Nick was able to anticipate his moves, and even though blocking them was just as painful as taking the hit, he was able to keep the guy at bay. Nick finally managed to land a kick to the guy's chest, sending the agent flying backwards. Before the guy could get up, Nick pounced on top of him and fired hit after hit until the guy's body went limp. Nick quickly leapt back up and readied himself for another onslaught. The fight raged for what felt like hours, but Nick knew it had only been minutes. His muscles were feeling fatigued, and his mind was sluggish from the hits he had taken from his last two opponents. He had been able to fall both of them, but he was beginning to worry if he could continue to fight. Battling Austin and Jared had helped prepare him, but everyone fought differently and taking on these new opponents was wearing him down. Add to it the fact that it was always in the back of his mind that he had to keep his back to the rock, and he was mentally exhausted.

A movement caught his attention to his far left. An agent had gotten past them and was headed toward the house. Nick dodged a hit from the guy he was fighting and then landed an uppercut into the guy's abdomen.

"We got a stray," he yelled, hoping someone could break away and get to the guy before he made it inside to the girls.

Everyone was enthralled in his own battle. Austin was taking on two agents at once, Jared was in a headlock and Adrian had one agent at gunpoint. Nick took a kick to his side; the pain that shot through him told him one or maybe even more of his ribs had just had more than it could take for the day and had broken from the impact. He sucked in a breath and tried to keep his legs from giving out.

"Adrian, shoot him!" Nick yelled.

Adrian's eyes shot over to Nick, and the guy Adrian had been holding at gunpoint immediately reacted; he snatched the gun from Adrian and shot him. Adrian crumpled to the ground.

"Fuck!" Nick roared.

Another gunshot rang out and Nick looked around to see who had been hit. He was surprised when he saw the agent who had just shot Adrian was laid out on the ground. Additional rounds filled the fight, and it finally registered that it was the sound of Hannah's Judge going off. When the man he had been fighting took a shot in his chest, Nick turned to find Hannah on the roof of the house, taking out super agents like a fucking professional.

Suddenly everything fell into slow motion. Nick felt a whoosh of air on his back, as dread settled in his belly. He had left his back unprotected. A strong arm wrapped around his neck before he could react. Nick fell into his Krav Maga motions, but the agent's grip was too strong and his pain tolerance too great. No matter how many times Nick elbowed the man in the gut, his hold around Nick's neck never lessened. Hannah screamed. Nick felt lightheaded from the pain and lack of oxygen. He threw his arm out trying to motion her to look away. He tried to scream at her to leave, but her eyes refused to leave his. She raised her gun and leveled it. Nick knew what she was going to do. He tried not to brace himself and just let it happen, but he couldn't resist. His body was exhausted from the pain, and the thought of more seemed impossible to survive. She pulled back the hammer and fired.

Chapter Thirty

Hannah

Nick fell forward along with the agent behind him. Hannah turned and crawled back through the window of the house. Just as she was about to stand up, she heard a man's voice in the living room below her talking to Nikki. Hannah held still.

"Where is she?" The man yelled.

Nikki didn't respond. Hannah could only assume the man was looking for her. She needed to get to Nick, regardless of what this man's agenda was. She stayed on her hands and knees and slowly crept forward on the balcony. She couldn't see the man, but Nikki, however, was in full sight, she had her arms up in surrender. Hannah hoped Nikki wouldn't see her and give her up. Hannah continued to slowly move further out onto the balcony. She was almost out where she needed to be to hopefully get a good shot off when Nikki's eyes flew up to hers. The man flipped around in front of Nikki. Hannah jumped up and trained her gun on the guy.

"You can't shoot me without shooting her," he said with a smirk, jerking Nikki in front of him.

What he didn't know was that Nikki was just far enough over so that Hannah could in fact shoot him. Hannah didn't say anything just smiled seconds before she pulled the trigger.

"I was hoping you were a good shot," Nikki said as she nervously jumped over the man's body and met Hannah in the middle of the living room.

"Are you okay?"

"I'm fine. He was looking for you."

"I figured that out. I have to go outside. I had to shoot Nick."

"What?"

"He was about to be suffocated to death, so I shot through him to shoot the guy behind him. Come on."

Hannah opened the door onto the deck and checked to see if there was anyone there before they ventured out. She slid down the side of the house, with Nikki right next to her until she got to the corner. They could hear the fighting, and Hannah's heart was racing, but she had to get to Nick.

"You don't have to go out there with me if you don't want to," she said as she turned to Nikki.

"Like hell, I don't."

"Okay."

Hannah looked around the corner quickly. No one was looking in their direction. Austin and Jared were fiercely outnumbered, but they seemed to be holding their own. Hannah slowly moved forward, trying to stay low, so she could use the coverage of the big rock to slip over to where Nick was lying. She managed to make it to Nick without being seen but just as she knelt down next to him, Jared saw her. His eyes hardened; obviously pissed that she was out there. Jared made quick work of the guy he was fighting and then moved closer to Hannah.

"Get the fuck back inside!" He roared.

"No. I'm helping him so just get over it," she yelled back.

Hannah quickly felt for a pulse on Nick. It was weak, but there. She let out a relieved breath as she then searched for the bullet hole. She had hit him right where she had meant to. It should be minimal damage for him, but she needed to stop the bleeding. Jared must have read her mind because he tugged his shirt over his head and tossed it to her before he met his next opponent in a clash of fists. Hannah ripped the shirt and covered the exit wound and the entrance and then pressed down hoping she could keep it at bay until they could get Nick to a hospital.

"Nikki, take my gun."

"No way!"

"You need to take it, just point and pull the trigger. We need protection, and I need to keep pressure on Nick."

"How about I put pressure on Nick, and you handle the gun part."

Hannah didn't like leaving it up to someone else to care for Nick, but if Nikki wasn't comfortable with a gun, Hannah knew it was best. She reluctantly pulled back from Nick and let Nikki take over. She placed herself in front of Nikki and Nick and held her gun up, ready to defend them. The ground was littered with bodies; Hannah wasn't sure if they were dead or just unconscious. Jared and Austin didn't look winded and were still fighting strong. The number of opponents was dwindling. One of them began to approach Hannah, she trained her gun on him, hoping he wouldn't make her shoot him. He continued straight for her, so she shot him in the leg.

"Hannah, we're going to have to do something soon with Nick," Nikki said from behind her.

"Damn," Hannah growled.

Hannah wanted to yell out to Austin or Jared, but she was too afraid she would distract them. She knew she wouldn't be able to get Nick to a vehicle on her own, and the second she put her gun down she would be attacked. The only thing she could do was wait. As Jared finished his fight, that only left Austin and the three men he was battling. She figured Jared would go help Austin, but instead he made his way over to Hannah.

"He needs help; fast," Hannah said to Jared.

"I'll carry him. Let's go."

"What about Austin?" Nikki said, fear lacing her words.

"He'll be fine, Nikki."

"I'm staying here," Nikki demanded.

"No. You'll be a distraction. Let Austin do his thing, besides after those three, there's no more left."

"What if some of these men begin to wake up?" Nikki asked.

Jared didn't say anything, but his face suggested the men were in no shape to simply wake up. Hannah didn't want to know; all she cared about was getting Nick help.

By the time Jared got Nick to the truck, and they got the truck keys, Austin had finished the fight. He ran over to them just as they were about to leave; he was carrying Adrian. Hannah hadn't even realized she hadn't seen Adrian fighting. Nick was spread out across the backseat of the truck, so there wasn't really any room for Adrian. Nikki jumped out of the truck and ran into the house. When she returned she had the keys for the truck that was parked in the garage. They hadn't used it since they had been there, so Hannah wasn't sure if it even ran. Thankfully it started right up, and they were all on their way to the hospital. Hannah continued to hold pressure on Nick's wounds as best as she could. She whispered to him the entire trip, begging him not to leave her. Every now and then Jared would glance back at her in the review mirror. Something almost like déjà vu settled over her, giving her an eerie feeling.

Chapter Thirty-One

Jared

Just as dusk was setting, they made it to the hospital with gusto, and both Nick and Adrian were whisked into surgery. Hannah nearly collapsed as they took Nick back through the doors. Jared had to eventually go get her and urge her back to the waiting room. They all looked a mess. He and Austin were covered in blood. Jared didn't even have a shirt on, but luckily Austin had found one in the truck for him to wear. They all settled into the waiting room. Austin was on the phone most of the time coordinating with one of his other government agencies to deal with the mess that was left in the back yard. With the bodies of the agents and the information Adrian had been gathering on Hornerstern, Austin convinced his friend in the FBI to handle the takedown of Hornerstern.

They were surprised to learn that Hornerstern had vanished. Jared could tell Austin was itching to go hunt the man.

"Want me to go?" Jared asked.

"No, for now we stay. Hornerstern's just digging himself a deeper grave by running," Austin said, exhaustion showing in his eyes.

"If he ran, he must have known his army had failed," Jared speculated out loud.

"Which means either he was close enough to see, *or* he had someone feeding him information."

"Fuck, what a nightmare."

Austin nodded but neither of them said another word. Austin would slip out of the waiting room to take phone calls periodically but otherwise they simply waited. Nikki fell asleep at one point, and Austin dozed off and on. Jared urged Hannah to sleep, but she refused. He tried to get her to eat, but she would just shake her head at him. He felt helpless. As dawn approached, Hannah stood up and stormed to the nurse's station demanding information on Nick. They hadn't been updated all night, and Jared tried to reassure her, but she wasn't having any of it.

The nurses assured her no news was good news, and that the doctors were still working. Hannah didn't seem completely appeased, but she sat back down nonetheless. When sleep finally captured her, she slumped over onto Jared's shoulder. His heart clenched as he adjusted her, praying she'd stay asleep now that he had her laid out across his lap. He smoothed her stray curls away from face as he took in her features. He had seen them a million times, studied them to the point of total memorization, but it felt like it had been forever since he had been so close to her. Since she had lost all memory of him, she didn't let Jared close to her at all; she barely could tolerate him in the same room. It felt like heaven having her snuggled against him.

Austin's phone buzzed again. Jared watched as Austin took the call. He could tell by Austin's features that whatever he was being told was important.

"Well," Jared probed as Austin sat back down.

"They got Hornerstern."

Jared waited because even though that seemed like good news, it looked as if Austin had more to say.

"He was at that dumpy motel in town. He's talking crazy; they're institutionalizing him until he can be fully debriefed and stand trial. Several of the agents lived."

"How many are several?"

"Enough to make a unit," Austin said, his eyes finally making eye contact with Jared.

"Fuck me."

"Yep."

They were interrupted by the doctor coming into the room. Jared gave Hannah a little shake when the doctor called for Nick's wife. The title made him physically sick to his stomach, but he powered through not only for Hannah, but also for Nick. Hannah rubbed the sleep out of her eyes when he finally got her awake. When she finally focused in on him, he could have sworn he saw recognition there, but when the doctor called for Mrs. MacKenzie again, she jerked away and jumped up to speak with the doctor.

"Your husband has made it through the surgery. He has two broken ribs, the damage from the gunshot wound is minimal, but it's still a very large wound, so it'll take some time to heal. Other than that, he's a bit dehydrated, so none the worse considering what he's been through."

"Thank you, doctor. May I see him?"

"Of course, but just you, and just for a minute."

Before the doctor could get out of the room entirely, Austin stopped him and asked about Adrian.

"I'm afraid he's still in surgery."

Hannah turned to leave with the doctor, her eyes briefly meeting Jared's again. He wanted to chase after her and ask her a million questions, but he didn't. For all he knew he could have just been imagining the entire thing, so he sat back down and waited. He wasn't sure why. Hannah would stick around for Nick, as would Austin, but Jared no longer had anything to wait around for. Hannah had made her choice. Hornerstern was caught and no longer a threat. Jared was a free man. He stood up and even though he knew he needed to go, he couldn't seem to put one foot in front of the other.

"Leaving?" Austin questioned from behind closed eyes.

"Trying."

Austin didn't say anything in return. Jared took a deep breath and let it out trying to focus. The doctor had called for Mrs. MacKenzie, and Hannah had gone. That was it. She wasn't Mrs. Tully, nor did she ever want to be. There wouldn't be any more runs together or chocolate chip pancakes for breakfast. No more stupid television shows that he hated but loved to pester her about.

Jared took a step.

There's was no more laughter or passionate kisses where his hand threaded through her perfectly, imperfect hair. No more hearing her moan his name when they were making love. There was nothing left of Jared and Hannah.

He walked to the door of the hospital. At some point in the night, it had started to rain. Jared looked back toward the door Hannah had disappeared through, but she wasn't standing there calling for him to come back. She wouldn't be chasing after him. Hannah was where she wanted to be; maybe where she had always wanted to be.

Finally, Jared found the courage to leave.

Chapter Thirty-Two

Nick

"I can walk, you know?" Nick chastised Austin.

"I know. I'm just here for support," Austin said from directly behind him.

Nick rolled his eyes. He was glad to be discharged from the hospital, but everyone was treating him like an invalid. Hannah had mothered him all morning. She meant well, and he was thankful to have her by his side, but he was ready for things to be normal. He finally made it to the couch and sat down.

"See, I made it all by myself."

"We can't help it if we care," Hannah said with a soft smile as she sat down next to him.

Nick noticed there was something different about her smile lately. He just figured it was because of his injuries, but it almost seemed worse now that they were home. Austin and Nikki said their goodbyes and took off.

"I'm going to get a hold of the place that has Presley and see about getting him picked up," Hannah said, standing up.

"Hey, come here for a second."

She sat back down, her eyes scanning the room as if she was looking for something. They didn't settle on Nick when she passed over him to look back at the foyer.

"You remember him, don't you?" Nick asked, his mind finally accepting what his heart had known from the minute he had opened his eyes up at the hospital.

Hannah had been sitting next to him, holding his hand but her eyes looked as if they were a million miles away. Nick had kept up an entire mantra of excuses for the distance he sensed between them while he had been in the hospital. All those excuses fell away now, staring at her tear-filled eyes. The house, their house once upon a time, now served as a reminder to her of Jared.

"I, um, no… I mean, I guess I remember," she said softly, as she wiped the tears from her face.

Nick captured one of her tears on his finger and pulled her against his chest. He placed a kiss on top of her head, inhaling her fragrant scent.

"You're the love of my life; my forever, but I can't be yours," he whispered.

Hannah sobbed against his chest.

"You remembered at the hospital, didn't you?" He asked.

She nodded her head, still buried in his chest.

"Why didn't you say anything?"

Hannah pulled back and grabbed Nick's hand, holding it tight.

"Because you were injured, and I had been so adamant about everything while I was under the influence of that serum I didn't know what to do or think. I still love you."

Nick didn't say anything as he continued to wipe the tears from her eyes.

"Somewhere along the way, Nick, my love for you has changed. I'm so sorry. When Jared and I were fighting about me not remembering him I asked him why I chose him, and he said he didn't know why. I never told either of you why. If I'm being honest, it's because I didn't want to make a final decision. I couldn't stand it if one of you walked away from me. That's so selfish. I'm so sorry; that wasn't fair to you or Jared."

"Hannah, nothing you could do or say will make me mad."

"That's just it. You're so forgiving and kind. I don't deserve it, but you deserve an answer. I chose Jared because he healed my heart and soul in a way I didn't think was possible. I chose him because he pushes me to better, and he accepts me when I'm not. When I look back on my life, all I see is you. The stupid things we did when we were kids, and the bliss we shared when we first got married, but when I look to my future, I don't see you. I don't know if it's because of the lies or just how the lies changed me, but there's a definite line in my life where you end, and he begins."

Even though Nick's heart was breaking, and it felt like his soul was physically separating from Hannah's as the words poured out of her, he also felt happy. Happy for Hannah, that she had finally made a choice. He knew she had been torn up for too long over the triangle they had created. When she finally stopped, her tears had quit falling, and she looked lighter than she had in weeks.

"I'll always be there for you. If you ever need anything, I'm simply a phone call away," Nick said.

"Nick…"

"Sh. It's okay Hannah. This has always been your choice to make. As long as you are happy, that's all I need to be happy. I hope you won't hate me for taking advantage of the extra time the serum gave me."

"Never because it gave me that extra time, too. I do love you, Nick, and that time will always be special to me."

Nick pulled out his phone and texted Austin. A few minutes later, Austin texted back with an address for Jared. Nick showed it to Hannah.

"Are you sure?"

"Go, Hannah."

Hannah kissed him hard on the forehead. Nick felt the tears there, or maybe they were his own, he wasn't sure. Hannah pulled back and took his face in her hands as they silently took each other in. Nick kissed her on the forehead briefly and then stood up and made his way to the bathroom, knowing he couldn't watch her walk out the door. A few silent minutes ticked by, and then he heard the small click of the door shutting behind her.

Nick made a phone call and then packed his bags. He walked out of the house for what he knew would be the last time. The day he had walked out on Hannah had been one of the hardest because he had been torn between two lives: the life he wanted to live with her and the life he lived amongst the shadows. He had walked the line between the two for too long. His phone buzzed in his pocket.

"I just got the call. You took the job."

"Yep. Are you resigning or sticking with me?"

"If I can survive living under Hornerstern's thumb for all those years, I suppose I could work for a guy like you," Austin joked.

"Good, I'll need you to get these new enhanced agents whipped into shape."

"Hannah?"

"She's happy. I'll see you Monday morning, Agent."

"See ya, boss."

Chapter Thirty-Three

Jared

Jared dropped the weights he had been lifting to the ground. Nothing seemed to wear him out anymore. Every time he closed his eyes, he saw her. Hannah consumed his mind every second of the day. No matter how many days passed, he couldn't seem to shake her. Every time he talked to Austin, he wanted to ask about her, but he didn't. He didn't think he could stand to hear her name. Jared slammed the door to his basement and went straight to his fridge for a bottle of water. He kept telling himself he was having such a bad day because he knew Nick was going home from the hospital. That meant Nick and Hannah would be back to their life.

He chugged the water and then threw the empty bottle on the counter. He didn't need water, he needed booze; lots of booze. The thing that haunted him the most was the look in her eyes when she had woken up at the hospital. He swore she looked as if she remembered, but that only made matters worse. If she had remembered him, then she had simply chosen not to contact him. Jared took a cold shower and threw a pair of jeans on. Just as he was heading to his bedroom to grab a shirt, his doorbell rang.

"Go away!" He yelled.

He had no idea who would be at his door, but his only guess was that it was more than likely Austin. He didn't want or need any more reminders of Hannah. The knocking continued, though, so Jared stormed over to his door and threw it wide. "What do you want?" He demanded before he realized who was at his door.

"I remember," she said.

Jared knew he was standing there like an idiot with his mouth wide open staring at

Hannah. He drank in the sight of her. She was just as beautiful as always in a pair jeans and a t-shirt, her hair flowing wild down her back. Her eyes were puffy from tears, which was what finally jerked him out of his stupor.

"What?"

"I remembered everything at the hospital."

Jared's heart soared but then quickly sank. If she remembered at the hospital, his suspicions had been correct. She had chosen Nick, and she must have shown up today out of pity.

"You know, it's fine, Hannah. We don't have to have this conversation. Please, just go," he said, as he began to shut the door.

"I never told you why I chose you," she said, catching the door and holding it open.

"I don't think it matters much now."

"May I come in?" She asked.

"I suppose."

She walked just inside of the door and looked around. His house was definitely a bachelor pad. Jared knew he shouldn't care, but he wondered what she thought of it.

"I love your strength; not just physically but emotionally. It inspired me and sometimes it was the only reason I'd get out of bed in the morning. I love your endurance; you push yourself to go further and do more. Sometimes that was the only thing that kept me wanting more for my life than what it had become. I love your loyalty; you're fiercely protective of the people around you. I love your smile and how it can brighten my entire being on even my darkest of days. I love your chocolate chip pancakes; especially when you shape the chocolate chips like a heart. I choose you for all of those reasons and more. I chose you because you're the line in the sand for where my past stopped dictating my life and allowed me to begin building my future; my future that I hope is with you. I chose you because I honestly believe every part of you was made to compliment every part of me. We just go together. I love you, Jared Tully; you're it for me."

She took a deep breath when she was done, as her eyes searched his. It took Jared a minute to process what she had said and what was happening. It was almost as if he needed to pinch himself to make sure he wasn't just imagining it all.

"I get it's presumptuous of me to just show up here and assume that after everything we've been through you'd still feel the same. I said some terrible things while I was under the influence of that serum…"

"Hannah, stop. Just shut up for a second."

Hannah stopped talking. Jared noticed she was wringing her hands together, so he laid one of his hands on hers. Tears brimmed her eyes, so he did the only thing he could think of that would make them both feel better. He kissed her. He poured his heart into the kiss. Every soul crushing moment of their separation, every ounce of love he felt for her, all poured into their kiss as his mouth slanted over hers demanding she give him the same. Hannah returned it with equal passion wrapping her arms around his neck and drawing herself close to him. His hands wrapped around her back and grabbed her ass, lifting her, so she had wrap her legs around his waist.

"I love you, woman," Jared growled as he tore his lips from hers.

"I love you, too."

Jared turned and walked them over to his kitchen table where he laid her down. He dragged his hand through his hair as he looked her over again. She sat up and took her shirt and bra off. His blood surged to his growing erection as the air left his lungs. She started to unbutton her pants, but he stopped her; he laid her back and finished undressing her himself. Once she was naked, his hands roamed all over her body. He had memorized every beautiful curve of hers before, so feeling them again was like driving down a familiar road; he barely had to look, he could navigate it by feel and memory alone.

He replaced his hands with his mouth as he began to kiss and nibble at her soft flesh. Jared slowly made love to her breasts, her nipples hardening under his tongue. Anxious to taste her, he ran a trail of open mouth kisses down her body until he reached her core. Her wanton scent overwhelmed his heightened senses. Hannah threaded her fingers through his hair and moaned his named as he devoured her sensitive bud. She quickly found her climax, screaming out his name.

Jared aligned himself with her opening slowly rubbing the tip of his erection back and forth across her wet slit. Hannah writhed under him. Jared gently grabbed her face and held her eyes captive.

"This is it for me, Hannah. Never again will another man touch you. Never again will another man taste you. I'm going to marry you, change your name, and then we're going to fill this house with babies. If that's not what you want, speak now."

"There's just one thing," she whispered.

Jared's heart skipped a beat as he nodded for her to continue.

"I'd like for all of that to happen as quickly as possible. I'm ready to be Mrs. Tully. I'm ready to raise our babies together, and mostly I'm just ready to be yours."

Jared slowly filled her, letting each inch be slowly devoured. It was excruciating and intoxicating all at the same time. Their eyes remained locked on each other. Once he was fully embedded inside of her, he stilled himself and let the pleasure of their union wrap around him. Hannah's hips bucked underneath of him urging him to move. He slowly pulled back out and then pistoned himself back inside of her. Hannah met his every thrust, until his slow and steady turned into a passionate frenzy. He pounded himself inside of her until he felt her tighten around him.

"Come, Hannah," he demanded.

She cried out in ecstasy as she spasmed around him, sending him into his own release.

Epilogue

Hannah

Five years later

"Don't you dare jump off that, Theo!" Hannah yelled at her toddler son seconds before he was about to jump off the top of his playhouse.

"He'd land it," Jared laughed.

"Don't encourage him," Hannah said smacking Jared in the stomach.

Jared grabbed his stomach and faked a painful look. Hannah rolled her eyes. The enhancement serum never wore off, so the man was virtually impossible to hurt. He and Austin still trained together regularly even though Jared had walked away from the agency. Austin had chosen to stay mostly to support Nick, but Hannah had a feeling that Austin and Nikki would be making an announcement soon that would more than likely change Austin's mind. Hannah couldn't be sure, but Nikki had a glow about her that was almost unmistakable.

"Come on, Theo. Let's go open up your presents!"

Everyone filed inside Hannah and Jared's new house. Theo bounced all the way to the kitchen and jumped up in the chair in front of his dinosaur cake. The boy was obsessed with dinosaurs. He spent most of his days playing with them or learning about them. He could tell Hannah all their correct names, and even corrected her if she dared to get one wrong. Hannah wouldn't trade her days with him for the world. Before too long she hoped that Theo would be an older brother. She and Jared had decided to wait before getting pregnant to give themselves time to heal after everything they had been through. They had also been curious to see if there was any of Jared's enhanced DNA passed down to their child. The doctor had worked tirelessly on trying to give them an answer, but it all boiled down to trial and error. Theo didn't show any signs of enhancement so far in his short life, but there was still a chance. Hannah prayed that the day would never come, but if it did, she knew it was something she and Jared would face together.

Jared lit the candle on the birthday cake, and everyone belted out the Happy Birthday song while Theo clapped along excitedly. Hannah looked around at the room full of people. Jared didn't have any family, but Hannah's family had welcomed him with open arms. Her father and Jared had become close friends, which worked out perfect since Theo's favorite person was also her father. The three of them were almost inseparable.

"Mommy, I open my presents?" Theo said after devouring his chocolate cake.

"Yes, but let's do something with that face first," Hannah laughed.

"No, don't want you to clean my face," Theo pouted.

Hannah just laughed but as soon as she approached him with the wet paper towel, he darted off. She chased him down and tackled him to the floor in a fit of laughter. Jared swooped Theo up from her grasp, face only partially cleaned, and took off with a laughing Theo over his shoulder.

"Hey, no fair!" Hannah yelled after them.

"Come on Mom, I think a three-year-old can open his birthday presents with a little chocolate on his face," Jared teased Hannah.

Hannah just laughed and caved. When her boys ganged up against her, she was helpless to their charm. Jared sat Theo down in the middle of his stack of presents and then made his way to stand next to Hannah. Jared leaned in and kissed her on the temple before tugging her into his side. She fit against him perfectly. They may have met in unusual circumstances and endured more than some couples could ever endure, but they were right where they were supposed to be; together.

"You're going to kill Austin when you see our gift," Nikki said.

"Oh no, what did he do?" Hannah laughed.

Nikki turned and pointed off the porch where Austin was unloading a battery operated four-wheeler.

"Are you serious?" She chastised Austin when he came back inside.

"Absolutely! Every little boy needs a four-wheeler."

"He's three, Austin."

Hannah looked to Jared for back up in her frustration, but his eyes were already sparkling with excitement, so she knew she was on her own. Jared smacked her on the butt lightly before taking off down the steps and joined Austin and Theo with the motorized death-mobile.

"Sorry, I tried to talk him out of it," Nikki said.

"That's okay. I suppose I should get used to it."

"You can pay us back when the time comes," Nikki whispered.

Hannah's eyes got wide as she looked at Nikki knowingly. Nikki held her finger over her lips, as a gigantic smile spread across her lips. Hannah let out a small squeal. "Does he know?"

"Not yet. I'm going to tell him tonight. I wanted to be sure. Five pregnancy tests and one blood test from my doctor's office later, I'd say it's a definite."

Hannah laughed. She could remember when she took her first pregnancy test with Theo. Hannah had gone a week with a newfound love for tomatoes and a heightened sense of smell before she thought to even take a test. She had peed through an entire pack of tests before it had finally sunk in. Jared at been at work, but when he came home she had laid out all three tests on a towel on the kitchen table. He stared at them for what had felt like hours. When he finally looked up at her, tears had brimmed his eyes, and he had the sweetest smile on his face. It wasn't something Hannah would soon forget. Her heart warmed every time she thought of it.

"Mom!" Theo yelled yanking her back to the present.

He was driving the four-wheeler around the front yard with Presley right behind him. Presley had gray on his muzzle, but that didn't stop him from trying to keep up with Theo's every move.

"How about we get to the rest of these gifts, mister," Hannah said, looking more at Jared than Theo.

She knew Jared was going to have to force Theo off his new ride.

"Oh, come on, he can open the rest later; let him ride," her dad said, always coming to her son's defense.

"I'm completely outnumbered," Hannah laughed.

"Get used to it, honey," her mom said.

"Do we at least have a helmet?"

Everyone was too enthralled to pay her any more attention, so Hannah made a mental note to add a helmet to her shopping list. That and lots of extra Band-Aids.

The rest of the day was spent watching Theo ride his four-wheeler and kissing his boo-boos when he'd crash. Hannah was still leery of the thing, but she had to admit Theo's smile when he was on it was making it worth it. After everyone left, and Jared and Hannah had finally dragged Theo inside, he opened up the rest of his gifts. They ooed and awed at all of his new dinosaurs and trucks, and Hannah made a note of who got what, so she could thank them later or send them a picture of Theo playing with it. There was one gift that didn't have a card, though. Hannah searched the bag and went over everyone who had come and who hadn't come and there was no one left.

"Jared, did you see who brought this bag in?"

"No, why?"

"I can't figure out who it's from."

"My present!" Theo demanded.

"Okay," she said, handing it over to him.

Theo ripped the tissue paper out of the bag and pulled out a Jurassic World themed helmet. Hannah instantly knew whom the gift was from. She looked up at Jared, just as realization set in for him as well. Jared smiled at her.

"Mom! Mom! Look, it's T-Rex! Mom! It's T-Rex!" Theo shouted excitedly as he plopped it on his head.

"I see that, buddy, it's awesome! I love it!"

Theo raced through the house pretending to drive with his new helmet on his head. Hannah stood up and went over to hug Jared. He held her tight as they watched Theo run around excitedly.

"It's the first bit of contact he's made," Hannah finally said.

"He may not make contact, but he's always there, watching over you and now Theo."

"Is that weird?"

"No, if there was ever anyone in this world I'd want watching over my wife and child, it's Nick. Without him, I wouldn't have either of you, so I'll be forever grateful to him."

"I just hope he finds his own happiness one day."

"Give it time. For now, let's just enjoy ours."

"Always."

"I love you, Hannah."

"I love you, too, Jared."

Want to know more about the author, keep flipping...

Other Books by Author

Hidden Series (Novellas)

Hidden Agendas

Hidden Enemies

Hidden Allies- Coming Soon

Power Duet (Novellas)

Exchange of Power

Weight of Power

Standalones

Retribution

Hardwired

Photo Credits to Autumn Dobbs of For Keeps Sake Photography

Andrea is a wife, mother and writer from small town, West Virginia. She spends her time while she's not dreaming up lovers and villains chasing after her two toddlers, three dogs and husband.

Her overactive imagination keeps her busy with ideas for new characters and stories.

Guilty pleasures include reading all night and Reese's Cups.

Stay In Touch

Facebook:
www.facebook.com/authorandreabills

Newsletter:

www.andreawillwriteforchocolate.wordpress.com

Email:

Author_abills@yahoo.com

Made in the USA
Columbia, SC
15 September 2019